Songbird

Kel Bruem

For my past self
You did it, baby.

CONTENTS

Content Warnings

As always, I believe the power of a content warning is it allows us to best prepare ourselves for the hard road ahead. Chris and Sarah's story deals with serious mental health and traumatic life events, that might hurt or surprise readers if caught unaware. Some possible triggering topics include: brief scenes of physical abuse, abuse of power dynamics between teacher and student, off-page parental death, post-traumatic stress disorder (PTSD) induced flashbacks, panic attacks, bullying, blackmail, and income disparity discrimination.

Chin up, shoulders back. You got this.

Sarah

There's a special kind of glow in the theatre, when the House lights dim and the stage lights come up, that makes me believe in magic. Actors move through the bubble of their imaginary world, unable to see the audience but feeding off the energy of 300 bodies hanging off every word that pushes from their diaphragm to bounce off the rafters. Plywood and paint become a bustling London avenue. Wigs shine and bounce as if they won't be pulled off and pinned to a mannequin in a few measly hours. Even footsteps sound different, striding confidently across wood flooring etched with scuffs, residue, stains of magic spells woven prior.

And if the players are spell casters, working their craft for three hours a night, six hours on weekends, then the crew is made up of alchemists, potions masters, creature whisperers, and overeager apprentices waiting for their chance with the wand.

That magic is why I used to commute two hours each way into the city for a job that barely pays any bills. It's why I waited and waited and waited for the housing lottery to finally call my name and it's why

I thanked the magic for landing me a studio walking distance from Contemporary American Theatre. That's why I was standing on a drafty stage at 3pm on a rare sunny San Francisco afternoon, palms sweating against my plastic three-ring binder with the script's front page waiting for my pen to begin its usual doodle-dance.

Not even luck could work that well.

I was thinking of the best metaphorically magical position for our director, already bracing myself for an argument with Angie about why she can't be a shapeshifter in the process, when the side doors swung open, sending in a blinding shaft of light across our dark.

Every head in the room swiveled as the muscled, broad-shouldered, overly chiseled form emerged. Chris Oldfelds, Hollywood heart throb and the latest star of The Captain Arrow Star superhero franchise, flashed the room a megawatt smile filled with *way* too many perfect teeth before whipping off his sunglasses to reveal sparkling blue eyes above crisp, deep smile lines.

Angie, my best friend and fellow production assistant, audibly gasped. Her blood-red spiked nails dug into my shoulder, her long raven black hair whispering against my arm.

"Sarah," she hissed. "He's *here*."

I pried her fingers off me one at a time. "Girl, it's call time. He better be here."

Although I was dead set on not losing my head over yet another movie star dallying in live theatre, there *was* something about Chris being CAT's original golden boy that had my stomach flipping. He'd apparently started out with CAT when he was barely out of high school, and an agent's girlfriend knew someone in the same show, so she dragged him to see it. The agent saw Chris, signed him, and married the girlfriend in an incredibly lavish ceremony thanks to all the insane movie money Chris was making them.

The entire cast and crew were gathered on the stage, waiting for our director, Alan, to start our first rehearsal. Whispers tore through the air, practically vibrating the floor as I watched Chris and Alan embrace. Alan was a thin, short man with round glasses that were constantly slipping to the end of his sharp nose. His hair was a mop of dark curls with two matching grey streaks along his temples. He exclusively wore band t-shirts beneath massive 80s knit sweaters from the thrift with cargo pants and sandals.

But that's not what I was staring at when the two broke their hug to do the manly "slap on the back" thing. An earnest tenderness had settled across Chris's face and for just that moment I could see the eager theatre kid he'd been at the start.

It did something to me—that look on his face. It tensed my shoulders, flipped my stomach, ran hot hands down my back. I had to pretend to be busy with my script until it passed. At that point, Alan was making housekeeping announcements.

Unfortunately, relief was short-lived.

"Sarah will be showing Chris around."

Crystalline blue eyes found mine from across the theatre, holding my gaze with more intensity than I was prepared for. It was all I could do to nod before ducking back into my binder.

Great, Sarah, really playing it cool with the visiting celebrity. Already, I heard the rest of the crew whispering to each other. A hot flush crept across my face and neck. Not for the first time I was grateful for Papi's melanin—at least it wouldn't be *obvious*.

"Thanks, Sarah," Chris finally said. "Hopefully the job will be easy for you. These are my old stomping grounds."

"The city has changed a lot since you've been gone," Alan said. "Sarah will be an excellent guide."

Chris looked like he wanted to say something else, but Alan clapped his hands together in that way he did—it was time to get to work.

"Act one," his voice boomed out across the space, ricocheting off the ceiling and slamming back into the wooden flooring. "Act One. Scene One. It's a quiet morning at the family estate..."

As he continued reading the rest of the stage directions, everyone leapt into a flurry of activity. Feet clamored and clacked into position, pages ruffled, throats cleared. I followed a few other crew members into the wings, rolling my eyes at Angie as she immediately looped an arm through mine, a knowing smile on her wine-red lips. But not even her teasing over my new celebrity "assignment" could dampen the welcome, familiar thrill that ran up my spine. Electricity jolted through my limbs as I flipped to the page in *Caught Red-Handed* where Alan was now. Although the pages were crisp and meticulous now, standing at attention in my binder, I knew they'd soon be wrinkled, torn, marked-to-hell with notes, stage instructions, reminders.

I couldn't wait.

"Tell me *everything*," Angie whispered, blowing me a kiss as she slid into the shadows of the wings, off to do whatever it was she did when she vanished like the theatre phantom.

The tell-tale sensation of eyes on me raised the hairs on the back of my neck and when I glanced around, I caught Chris Oldfeld's steady, bright gaze once more. I fixed him with a look I hoped communicated that I didn't *actually* care that he was famous—I could see him for who and what he really was. A big nerd a little too excited to get on stage in a historical communist drama.

He looked a little startled, but a charming half-smile crept up his sharp cheekbones. I couldn't help it. I flashed him a single, shy smile in return before turning back into the darkness of the wings.

CHRIS

"That's lunch, everyone!" Alan closed his folio with a soft thud. "Meet back here at 1:30 PM, we'll continue blocking. Chris, a moment?"

My body was hollow with hunger, a sensation I'd been ignoring while absorbed in the world of the play. But now it rang through me, demanding attention.

I stepped to the edge of the stage where Alan was looking up at me, his folio clutched to his chest.

"Let me take you to lunch," he said. "A little welcome back present."

I couldn't stop myself from glancing around, not sure who I was looking for until I landed on a flash of black curls rapidly disappearing out the back.

I nodded, trying to clear my head. "Is Frankie's still around?"

Alan laughed, throwing a sharp hand to the side exit. "Hollywood hasn't changed your appetite too much, I see."

"If I have to eat any more quinoa and kale, I'm gonna go crazy," I said, hopping off the edge of the stage to meet Alan in the aisle. "I've been daydreaming about their lunch special since I took the role."

"It'll just be a moment while I call a car." Alan squinted at his phone as we stepped out into the midday chaos of downtown San Francisco. The sun was making a rare appearance for this time of year, the usual late summer fog nowhere to be seen.

"Actually, would you mind MUNI?"

Alan looked at me over his square glasses, bushy eyebrows sporting the same salt and pepper of his hair.

"Of course not, so long as you don't."

I slid on my secret disguise: comically large sunglasses and a baseball cap with a curved brim I pulled down low across my forehead. "I'm ready for anything."

We made our way to the nearest stop for MUNI, the city's above-ground railcar. We didn't have to wait long before the two-car train pulled up, the familiar automated voice calling out the next stop as the doors whooshed shut behind us. Inside, people scrolled silently through their phones, not bothering to look up as Alan and I found seats near the back.

As much as smartphones had changed the mood of the city around us since I'd been gone, I was glad for the anonymity in the moment. I let the rare sunshine wash over us, taking in the buildings as they passed. Some storefronts hadn't changed, and I could envision a ghost of my younger self walking through these streets, daydreaming as he passed.

But some stores were completely gone, erased with trendy new white-washed stucco and big square windows containing neat, cursive neon signs that said quirky things unrelated to the wares being sold.

My heart leapt into my throat the closer we got to Frankie's. What if it had changed?

MUNI crested a sharp hill and then, at the resting point before the next big swell in the street, there was Frankie's. I let my breath go in a huge sigh, and Alan stood as the doors opened.

"Just as I remembered," I said, stepping onto the sidewalk and gazing at the brightly painted corner building. It was teal and dark blue, with the name scrawled across the far side in old-school building-height hand letters. The street that intersected where we stood gave a picturesque view of the city, brightly colored buildings reflecting the sunlight with a cheery glow.

Inside, Frankie's hadn't changed an inch—from the same dust-covered knick-knacks hanging on every free inch of faux dark wood wall to the cafeteria-style tables, peeling with age. Yellow lights hung above us, and a fan swung lazily in the middle of the space. I rubbed my hands together greedily.

"I'm going to need one of everything," I said, already drooling a little at the smell of brisket and roast wafting through the air. A roll of butcher paper advertised the day's specials, and I could see the carving board covered in fresh juices.

"Just remember you have to be able to stand up for the rest of the day," Alan said, waving at the girl behind the counter.

I ignored him and immediately ordered brisket, pulled pork, fried chicken, and a heaping portion of each side.

"You can prop me up with a dolly," I said, grunting as I set the heavy tray down on a table nearby. Everything was incredible—tender, flavorful, hearty. Exactly what I needed after years of special fitness diets and trendy brunches in Los Angeles.

"How does it feel to be back?" Alan asked, eyeing me over his modest roast beef sandwich and side salad.

"Weird," I said around a mouthful of chicken. "But I'm hoping that'll fade the longer I'm here."

"Are you planning on staying after the show closes?"

"Maybe," I shrugged. "It'll depend on what Steve calls me with, honestly." I tried to ignore the sudden sinking feeling in my gut at the thought of returning to movie sets so soon. We'd barely gotten started and already I was feeling more energized about my work than I had in years.

"We'd make sure there was something for you," Alan said, looking at his sandwich thoughtfully. He'd barely taken a bite. "If you were to stay."

I set down my chicken, choosing my next words carefully as I wiped my hands.

"Without putting anyone else out of work?" I asked. Usually, the season was set by now, with rehearsals for the opener overlapping rehearsals for the winter show. Auditions might open in the middle of the opener's run for the musical that usually debuted in the spring, but that would be it. If Alan made good on his offer, that would most likely mean bumping someone who had already been given a part.

Someone who didn't have movie money to fall back on.

Alan decided now he was hungry, taking several opportunistic, huge mouthfuls of sandwich. We sat in silence while he chewed and took a long drink of water.

"Alan," I prompted, arching my eyebrows. I wasn't going to let him get away with not answering.

"Nothing is set in stone, Chris," he said. "You know that, I know that, and everyone else in our industry knows that. Parts change, shows get cut—it's part of the thrill of our art."

I shook my head.

"At least consider it," Alan said, steepling his fingers together over our table and looking at me seriously. "We haven't been filling seats the last few years, and we're starting to feel the pressure of it. It's not like our rent has lowered. We could use someone exciting and universal like you to bring new people in. Imagine! You'd be the introduction to live theatre for so many young people."

"I hope you're right, for *Caught Red-Handed*," I said, tapping the table for emphasis. I wanted to pull Alan's focus back to the now—the future felt like too much to swallow. "I'm still worried that no one will show, like when we opened *King Lear*."

Alan laughed and picked his sandwich back up. "Thank God neither of us are twenty-two nor just starting out," he said.

I smiled back, unable to shake the same feeling I'd had at twenty-two when I thought about opening night. Ten years later, and I still got pre-show jitters just thinking about it.

But maybe that was what told me I was in the right job, that it never stopped making me nervous.

Only opening night would tell.

SARAH

"**Y**ou are literally the luckiest girl in the world," Angie whined, swinging shut the fridge door where the ready-made salads sat waiting for impatient businessmen to snag them on their way back to the office.

"I've got a leak in my kitchen that disagrees," I muttered, eyeing the sandwich counter in the back of the corner store. I'd packed yet another quinoa protein bowl for my lunch, but yet again, it was lunch time, and I didn't want it. I was dreading having the same lunch I'd had every day for a year straight. Amá had gone on a health kick, buying one monstrous bag of quinoa after another from Costco, showing up every six months to replenish. Some white lady had convinced her at work that her arroz y frijoles was making her fat and naturally that meant now I was getting fat, too. At least in my mom's eyes. And while I was proud of my thick thighs and round ass—I had curves that sent musicians and artists to their knees with the lived experience to prove it—I was also Mami's girl. I wouldn't waste food, and I wouldn't waste her effort and money.

Angie rolled her eyes at me. "Forget your sink, Sarah, you get to spend one-on-one time with *the* Chris Smolders!"

"Oldfelds," I corrected, cringing inwardly at her use of the tabloid nickname. An old fear was beginning to rear its head. One I hadn't felt in more than a decade and I wasn't enjoying the familiar wave of panic as it washed over me.

"Whatever," Angie paid for her salad, flipping the long, shiny wave of her black hair over her shoulder. She was a few inches shorter than me with dark eyes and more curves than most East Asian women I knew. And she didn't hesitate to throw them around to get what she wanted. "This is your chance."

"For what?" I sighed, shaking my head at the guy behind the counter. Yet again, I would not be buying the sandwich my heart desired. Angie and I stepped out into the honking, screaming, chaos that was downtown San Francisco, making the short journey back to the theatre's green room.

"You know 'for what,'" Angie said, mocking me lightly. "Show him what you can do!"

"Angie, no," I stiffened. One stupid night at the karaoke bar and now Angie wouldn't shut up about how I needed to be a singer. She'd signed me up for auditions, shoved me into teacher studios with no warning, and even gone so far as to arrange a broken-down elevator disaster with me and Alan. I loved my best friend's dedication and support, envied her ability to jump in and do whatever scared her, but sometimes she was aggressive.

"Ugh *Sarah*," she dropped her shoulders down, rolling her head back on her neck dramatically. "You have this incredible thing, and you won't do anything with it. It's infuriating."

"Angie. What if..." I shoved my hands in my pockets, suddenly aware of how tight my chest was growing, how hot I felt beneath my light jacket in the crisp San Francisco breeze. "I mean...you heard everyone whispering. I can't..." I let the words trail off.

Angie, sweet patron saint of my terrified heart, whirled on her heel, gripping my shoulders tightly and fixing me with a calm, confident look.

"Deep breath, hold it, now deep breath out." I followed her instructions, repeating the actions as she repeated the words. "Better?" I nodded, but she kept a firm grip on me, forcing the flow of pedestrians to push around us like a rock in a raging river. "Remember: you're not seventeen anymore. Those bitches are living in the suburbs with their miserable husbands and *you're* living your dream. Because *you* did the work. You followed your passion. You stick it out every year."

I nodded, embarrassed at the praise she showered me with—mortified that I couldn't seem to accept it as a truth rather than mollification.

"What was that phrase you taught me in Spanish? Chinga tu madre?"

I swatted at her shoulder. "Shhh, not so loud."

"Well, chinga tu madre at goddamn Mr. Thompson, anyway. Fucking pervert."

I giggled, feeling a little lighter as the panic slowly dissolved. She was right—I was ten years away from that disastrous senior year when *it happened* and the entire school turned against me, deciding for me that I'd been a willing participant in exchange for choir solos and leads in the school play.

"That's not really how that works," I said, smiling at Angie.

"It feels good to say it anyway," she said, finally releasing me from her grip. "Besides, all those bitches can eat your ass when *the* Chris Oldfelds tells the world how talented you are."

"It doesn't matter how good I am or not," I said, as we reached the theatre. I held open the side door for Angie as a new anxiety reared its head. My insides were already twisting as old ghosts crowded the sides of my vision. "I'd never be able to perform, so why bother?"

"Wait!" A male voice called from around the corner. As if the universe were playing some cruel joke, Alan and Chris walked toward us, Chris holding a hand up in greeting.

Before I could stop her, Angie waggled her eyebrows at me and swung the door shut. I heard the distinct click of the lock engaging, and I stifled the urge to scream at the sky.

"Was that Angie?" Alan asked as they reached me.

I sighed and nodded. "She locked the door," I said.

"That girl," Alan shook his head. "If I didn't know any better, I'd say she's trying to sabotage you."

"Don't be fooled, that's exactly what she's doing," I said, barely keeping the embarrassment from my voice.

"Your friend locked you out?" Chris asked and I could only glance at him momentarily before the heat flooded my face. He had *zero* business being that hot—chiseled jaw, angelic blonde hair swooped away from his kind face, blue eyes sparkling. It was actually *unfair* to the rest of humanity. He should have his nose cut off to even the playing field.

"She thinks she's being encouraging," I muttered at my dirty shoelaces.

Alan pulled on the door and knocked, rolling his eyes when Angie's muffled voice came through.

"Sing the password!"

"Ang, come on, we're gonna be late," I pleaded.

Alan opened his mouth like he would yell at all of us, but Chris cut him off, crooning out a perfect, Broadway-ready few notes where he inserted "password" for all the lyrics.

The door swung open, and Angie stuck her head out, eyes wide as spotlights.

"So unfair," she said, shaking her head at me. She held the door as I tried not to get caught sprinting away from Chris and Alan.

"Sarah, wait!" Chris called out after me, and I found myself stopped so suddenly in my tracks I nearly tumbled onto the floor.

I turned to see him lightly jogging to cross the distance between us in the back hall. His steps echoed off the cold concrete.

"Could you show me where the fridge is?" he asked, holding up a takeout container I hadn't noticed before. "I went a little overboard at Frankie's."

"*You* ate at Frankie's?" I was shocked, glancing over his rippling superhero chest.

He threw me a wink and I nearly died on the spot. Hot, charming, *and* he could eat?

"I'm still a San Francisco kid at heart," he said. "Captain Arrow Star or not."

I led him down the hall, hooking a right deeper into backstage. The green room had a mini fridge for snacks and drinks when actors needed them during performances, but I doubted Chris' massive takeout container would fit between the Diet Cokes and carrot sticks.

The big fridge where we kept lunches, drinks, and communal dinners leaned against the back wall of the set storage area. It was plugged into a rogue outlet, too high to be used for much else, the dirtied cord snaking up as if it were reaching for the ceiling.

I held my hand out for the container. "I can bring this back up to the House for you when you're done for the day," I said, sliding the hefty package along the metal slats of the fridge shelf. My quinoa was still sitting there in the same stained Tupperware I'd packed it in last night.

"Only if you promise not to steal my drumstick," he said, grinning. "I know how tempting Frankie's is."

A few more crew members were filtering into the room around us and I could feel their eyes on us, waiting for any action, whisper, meaningful look that would give them something to talk about later—something to use against me, I was sure.

Angie had said this wasn't the same situation anymore—I wasn't seventeen, I wasn't in high school, I wasn't surrounded by jealous bitches.

Right?

Before I could reign in my own protective instincts, I felt the low coil of my anxiety transforming into anger. Where the fuck did he get off trying to accuse me of stealing his leftovers? I knew the holes in my sneakers and the tear in my jeans didn't exactly scream "this bitch has cash" but I didn't think I looked so broke I deserved to be accused of stealing celebrity leftovers.

He was probably kidding but the sudden loud growl of my stomach made the jab sting more than I wanted to admit.

"I'll do my best to stay away from your lunch," I said, serene but cold and definitely loud enough that several heads in the room snapped toward us.

All Chris' Hollywood charm evaporated, and I found myself able to meet his gaze for the first time. A flicker of hurt flashed through his eyes as he peered out from underneath a near-perfect swoop of blonde hair. His megawatt, movie-hero smile faltered, causing one dimple to go into hiding, and I inwardly chided myself for my disappointment at its disappearance. Confusion crinkled his well-shaped eyebrows as his mouth pulled down at the corners.

I pulled out my Tupperware before letting the fridge swing shut. I wasn't excited about my lunch, but I'd cooked it myself. It was all I had, and that was good enough for me even if this star-studded himbo thought otherwise.

I brushed past Chris, walking back to the stage without another word.

Of course, he had an ego. There's no way he could have looks, charm, talent, *and* a great personality. Something had to give.

At least, that's what I told myself.

I found Angie in the seats, tidy notations already running down the margins of her script. Her convenience store salad was balanced across her knees, the fork hanging from the edge of her mouth. We were both working props for this show, which meant knowing the show better than the actors did so not a single thing was out of place when the time came.

"That was a dirty trick," I said, sitting next to her.

"You're welcome," she said without looking up. "I saw you got a little alone time with Smolders, too."

"You have to stop," I pleaded. "It's getting embarrassing. Even Alan knows what you're up to."

"Then he should give you the audition." Angie turned the page slowly with a well-manicured finger. They were blood red this week and pointed like talons.

The audition.

The lead for the spring musical had a family emergency across the country and dropped out at the last minute. They were actively auditioning for the role, but Alan was being particularly choosy about finding a replacement. No one knew why. Angie had decided it was because fate was waiting for me to take the opportunity. I really couldn't handle this push on top of all the other anxieties and emotions warring through me that afternoon. I was suddenly exhausted.

"I don't want the audition," I sighed.

"You don't want the chance to try out for your biggest childhood dream?" Angie shot me a look over the top of her binder.

"This is *not* Broadway," I hissed.

"It's still a live stage," she hissed back, clutching the binder to her chest and pointing her salad fork at me. "It's still singing in a professional show. How else do you think people get to Broadway, Sarah?"

"The union—"

"You aren't union," she said cutting me off. "This is your now or never chance."

She was right. Once I finished my hours and sent in my dues, I'd be accepted into the stage workers' union. Trying to make the leap from production assistant to actor would get a whole lot more complicated—or it would mean starting from scratch. But just like Angie had pointed out, I had worked too hard for too long for my career and the respect that came with it. I wasn't just some girl in choir that the director supposedly fucked—not anymore. I was doing this for real. And I wasn't eager to throw that all away because Angie had steep ambitions for me.

"But it's *my* chance. So, I get to decide if I take it or not," I said. Even the suggestion of taking the audition made my stomach tie itself further in knots.

"Not if I have anything to say about it."

Alan's thunderous clap startled us both, and Angie swiveled around to face him, continuing to munch on her salad.

"Alright, folks," he said. "Top of scene three, let's run it again just to be sure we have it."

CHRIS

Four grueling hours later, and we were finally done. Alan dismissed us, turning to talk intensely and immediately to a white man in his early 50s, wearing an expensive suit, hair expertly cut to display the streaks of grey washing through it. I watched the two of them for a moment, startled when the man whipped around and pointed directly to me and another actor, Nicole, who was playing my on-stage wife. She was a Black woman, built like Wonder Woman, tall and muscular with a commanding presence. She was exactly what the part needed, and I'd liked her immediately.

"You two." He pointed to the edge of the stage in front of him. We exchanged a nervous glance, and I wasn't encouraged by the flash of fear across her face. "This is what Hollywood money buys? Dropped lines, botched cues, and a leading woman so starstruck she can't carry a scene in a bucket?"

Alan cleared his throat. "Chris, I'd like you to meet Paul Vladik, our Artistic Director."

"Pleasure," I said, flashing him my camera-ready smile. It wasn't.

"Don't give me that. I told Alan I didn't want any stunt casting. We might not be selling out shows but we're not sell outs. Ya got me?" He arched thin eyebrows at me expectantly. My chest tightened, clamping down on already fast and shallow breathing. The world tilted dangerously and whatever Paul said next was lost to the cotton plugging my ears.

"Respectfully, no actor is perfect the first week." Nicole's voice floated over a tinny ringing in the background. She slipped a comforting hand in mine and squeezed. I tried to do the grounding exercises my therapist had taught me in preparation for coming to San Francisco—I could feel Nicole's hand in mine. I could smell the dust burning off the radiator backstage. I could see Paul staring at me in disbelief.

"Got you," I said, finally heaving a deep breath and feeling the world rush back at full-volume. I hoped I sounded more confident than I felt.

"Good. Dismissed." Paul waved his hands through the air and turned on his heel, marching up the vom and out of sight.

"What a dick," I sighed. Nicole squeezed my hand, offering a reassuring smile.

"We'll just have to prove him wrong," she said.

"We will," Alan chimed in. But I didn't miss the way he was white knuckling his folio.

The crew behind us was a flurry of activity, sweeping the stage and hauling furniture around at a lightning pace, resetting for tomorrow's rehearsal. I knew they'd be relieved that we were working with a skeleton set for now, meaning everyone would go home soon rather than remaining for another hour or so.

A few of the other actors offered me bright smiles and welcoming handshakes as they shrugged into coats and tied scarves, heading out into the chilly summer evening. I found myself lingering, hesitant to face the next step of this homecoming journey.

The apartment was waiting, and I wasn't ready. I could barely deliver lines—my *only* job—how was I going to face down the very apartment still haunted by Mom's ghost?

Alan noticed—of course Alan noticed—and before I could stop him, he had a hand in the air and was calling for Sarah.

"Would you be so kind as to escort Chris to his apartment? I believe it's in your neighborhood."

She looked from Alan to me and back, eyes wide, one eyebrow arched. Even her profile seemed to pull me in—the generous nose, her rounded cheeks, the tilt of her neck.

It wasn't an uncommon request—crew often showed out-of-town actors around so they knew where things were, what to order for lunch, how to get between their hosted apartment or hotel and the theatre. But I wasn't exactly an out-of-towner.

"Oh, Alan, I'm a big, tough, boy I can find my way," I joked, squeezing Alan's shoulder good-naturedly as I attempted to intervene.

Alan let out a small sigh and looked to Sarah, clearly about to dismiss her. She saw it coming and interrupted.

"I'd be happy to," she chirped. "Anything to help the show go smoothly." Did I imagine her glancing over her shoulder for the briefest moment?

Alan arched an eyebrow, but something shifted in his face. "Thank you, Sarah, it would be most helpful."

"And I'd appreciate the company," I grinned despite myself. "Let me grab my Frankie's, and we can head out."

I practically sprinted to the back of the theatre and into the warehouse-like green room where the crew fridge was plugged in. My heart was thudding in my chest and tingling excitement flipped my stomach.

Easy, buddy. You don't even know her yet.

And yet.

Without thinking, I grabbed a fistful of paper towels and plucked a chicken drumstick from my leftovers, holding it as if it were a fresh-picked daisy and not a greasy meat snack.

"Here," I said, embarrassed at how breathless I sounded, offering Sarah the perfectly fried chicken drumstick, the bone end wrapped in the paper towel. "A thank you for walking me home."

"I bet this wins over all the ladies in Hollywood," she said, giving me a skeptical look. But she accepted my offering, wrapping it entirely in the towel and tucking it into her own now-empty Tupperware.

"I usually lead with your basic nugget, and we work up to a drumstick," I said. "Consider this extenuating circumstances."

Jesus Chris, shut up.

But she smiled and my heart skipped a beat at the brilliance aimed in my direction. Alright, so maybe I wasn't so stupid.

"Where are you staying?" She asked, leading the way out the side exit. My answer was lost as the door opened onto a cacophony of screaming women, shouting reporters, and flashing lights popping off cameras. Before I could even think about panicking at the onslaught of paparazzi and fans, Sarah slammed the door, crushing a few microphones in the process.

"We're gonna take the back door," she said, as if she were making a suggestion to take the scenic route.

"You're surprisingly calm about this," I said, following her quick pace to the back exit. It opened on an unused alley that reeked of garbage and piss. The chain-link fence that separated the theatre from the apartment building next door pressed in impossibly tight, but it certainly avoided any extra attention, even if I wouldn't fit.

"Robert Downey Jr. did a show with us last year," Sarah said. "Anything after that guy is cake."

"Watch your step," Sarah continued, nodding at a monstrous puddle of piss. "That'll take a good scrub to get the stench out."

I managed a secure leap across it, but Sarah's shorter stature meant it was more difficult for her. She landed on wobbly legs. With nowhere else to go between the wall and my chest, her momentum carried her forward so she face-planted into my t-shirt.

I got a good whiff of her shampoo—something fruity and crisp—and my brain took off, imagining the lingering scent on my pillow as I rolled over in the morning. But my daydream was cut short by the unmistakable deep inhale of her face in my chest.

Was she smelling *me*?

"You alright?" I braced both hands on her shoulders and gave her a gentle nudge upright. I had no idea if the paps on the far side of the theatre knew about this alley, and I didn't want to have Sarah dragged through tabloids for sniffing me. When she looked up at me, I lost the ability to say anything else, realizing how close we were, the fence pressed against my back.

"Clumsy," She muttered. "Sorry."

She took off, leaving me to follow. We waited at the edge of the alley while she checked the coast was clear. I donned my aviators and Oakland A's baseball cap, pulling the brim low. Classic celebrity disguise.

"I assumed you were a Giants fan," she said, turning the corner and finally heading down the street away from the theatre.

"You kidding?" I couldn't help but scoff. "A's for life. My mom used to take me all the time when I was a kid."

She considered that for longer than I could stand, before finally changing the subject. "You never told me where we're going."

"1055 Pine Street."

She stopped dead on the sidewalk. "What did you just say?"

"Is there a problem?"

"Yeah, that's my building."

"How 'bout that, neighbor." I grinned, hoping it came across as sincere and not creepy or perverted.

"How did you swing that?" She asked. "There's *never* an opening in my building. Most of the tenants have had rent control for forty years."

"There must be one now," I said, hoping to gloss over the fact that I'd paid the current tenant an embarrassing sum if she'd sublet to me for the season. "Anyway, I'll be glad to have company for the commute. Do you drink coffee?"

"I usually make some before I leave for the theatre," she said, plainly. "I have a French press I'm obsessed with right now."

"I never mastered those. Mine always came out full of grounds."

"Are you putting the plunger on top of the grounds or vice versa?"

"Oh. Oh no." I laughed, embarrassed. "You know, I wondered if it was a French thing to chew the grounds. Maybe it had health benefits I didn't know about."

"Common mistake," she said, a half-smile creeping across her face. "Even in a world with Google."

"Stop." I covered my face with my hands, still laughing. "That's worse."

"Okay, okay." She was laughing now, and my stomach flipped at the sound. "Google couldn't help you anyway, don't worry about it."

"This is why I buy coffee every morning."

We resumed our walk, nearing the building.

"Okay, fancy," she teased.

"You should join me on the fancy side," I said, unable to look her in her bright eyes, finding the edge of my jacket to fiddle with for comfort. I had just asked the cute PA for a date, and we weren't even through rehearsals. Surely this was a bad idea.

"Oh, um." She seemed confused but considerate, as if I'd asked her to choose between two equally impossible but delightful choices.

"My treat," I said, finding her eyes and feeling my heart stutter as she asked a silent question.

"I'll make us coffee," she said, words tripping over each other.

We stared at each other for just a moment, but it felt like an hour.

"Deal," I said, letting my face break into a soft smile.

"Do you know your unit?" She asked, yet again abruptly changing the subject as we reached the building. It was a multi-level square marble building that looked painfully out of place next to its more charming, colorful, bay-windowed neighbors.

"310."

"Great," she said, clearly trying not to let the panic stretch her smile too far.

"Is that your apartment, too?" I asked, arching my eyebrows, barely able to hold back the laugh that was pressing against my teeth.

"You'll see," she said, leading the way up the stairs. "Did someone bring your stuff over for you?"

"Yeah, my assistant," I said without thinking.

"Your *who?*"

"Jess," I said. "But she's taking a few weeks off since I'm doing the show. It'll be less hectic while I'm here than it usually is on set."

"You're sure you're not a Giants fan?" She muttered, pushing open the heavy fire-safety door on the third floor that led to the main hallway.

We walked a short distance straight ahead, the ancient carpeting doing little to muffle our steps. Traffic wafted up to meet us through the thin walls, the shrieking breaks and horns a familiar ambiance. At the far end of the hall, a small window led to the fire escape, although the grime on its outside pane was so thick it let in very little light. The paint was scuffed to a light grey at shoulder height from so many bodies moving through the hall over the years, but I noticed a few tenants had taken it upon themselves to hang art.

Sarah stopped in front of 310—right next to a familiar Diego Rivera print.

"This is you," she said, pointing at the green door with flaking gold numbers.

"Are we neighbors?" I asked, unable to keep the hope from my face and voice. She paused, looking at me as if for the first time before letting out a long-suffering sigh.

"Yeah," she said, jerking a thumb over her shoulder at another identical door. "I'm 309."

"Amazing," I said, my smile breaking my face wide open. "This means I'll always have a buddy for the walk home."

"It sure does." She did *not* seem thrilled.

"I promise not to be weird about it," I added, holding my hands out for peace. "No knocking on your door in the middle of the night or peeping on your gentleman callers."

"How do you know it's gentlemen calling?" She arched a graceful eyebrow.

"Mea culpa," I said, placing my hands flat on my chest and splaying my fingers out. I was beginning to sweat lightly under my jacket. "Whosoever calls on the lady will mine visage escape."

"Wow, okay." She laughed. "Don't worry about it, Romeo. I guess I'll see you tomorrow then."

As we each turned to fumble with our keys, I realized my heart was hammering in my chest and my vision began to tunnel. The front door seemed suddenly too close and simultaneously too far away. When I reached for the handle, it shrieked and ground in the frame but refused to budge. I tried nudging it with my shoulder, tried lifting it and bracing myself against it, tried jiggling the handle one way then the other. Nothing.

This was my old apartment. This was my old home—the very same I'd shared with Mom before she got sick, before I moved her to LA, before that same illness carved her to mere bones and took her away to the only place I'd never be able to get her back from. Mom was dead, I was a hack, and I couldn't even open a *goddamn door*—

"You got it?" Sarah's voice floated over my shoulder as I tried to calm my erratic breathing.

"It's stuck," I gritted out.

"Here." A warm hand soothed my shoulder, nudging me out of the way. We were dangerously close now, with her soft curves pressed between me and the door.

"These doors are old and stubborn," she continued, lifting the knob while simultaneously pulling the door closer to the jamb. Then she turned and pushed with her shoulder until the door clicked open.

"You're magic," I whispered, unable to stop myself. I didn't imagine her wide-eyed gaze finding me over her shoulder, the soft drop of her lips into a surprised "O."

"Just lived in a lot of old places," she said, wiping her hands on her pants. "You good?"

Glancing past Sarah to the gaping mouth of the entryway, the apartment dark and silent, I felt suddenly lost. But this wasn't a journey Sarah could guide me through. No. I needed to take these steps alone.

"I'm great," I said, flashing what I hoped was another megawatt smile. "Thank you again. See you tomorrow. Thank you in advance for coffee."

"Con gusto," she practically purred and I thanked whatever deity was watching as she slid away from me and back across the hall. But before I could see to my emotional traumas and the erection that was growing more and more painful, Sarah stopped me again.

"Why did they put you up in *this* place?" she asked, interrupting my hesitant steps into the apartment.

"I requested it," I said, that sense of loss threatening to overwhelm me again. If I lingered any longer, I was going to lose my resolve. I was going to throw myself at Sarah's feet and plead with her to take me in, to save me from the grief I knew was waiting just on the other side of this darkness.

Instead, I gave her a quick wave before closing the door with a quiet click.

CHRIS

I turned away from the door, letting my eyes adjust to the dark. I was scared if I turned the lights on, I'd have to take everything in all at once before I was ready.

The door had new tricks. I hadn't expected that. I was sure my usual double-twist-lift routine would open it like it had all those years ago.

What else would be different?

I took careful steps into the apartment, passing the dark abyss of the kitchen where the time blinked from above the oven, a tiny green beacon.

The living room was dimly lit, the late afternoon sun slanting through cracks in the blinds. None of the furniture was ours, but I recognized the patch in the wall above the sofa, a relic from pretending I was a Ninja Turtle one Sunday afternoon. Mom was furious but used the opportunity to teach me how to repair a wall so a landlord would never notice.

"Why'd they put you up in this place?" Sarah's words still rung through my head. Maybe I'd tipped my hand too much by telling her

the truth. Now that I was a household name, people I thought I could trust were constantly running to the paparazzi to repeat everything I said to them.

I could see the headlines now: *Chris Oldfelds Ousts Tenant for Theatre Access.*

Then I remembered the way Sarah slammed the door on the microphones. For now, I figured I could trust her.

It'd been tricky explaining to Alan why I wanted to rent my family's old apartment—the place I'd grown up when it was just me and Mom. I told him I had some superstitions about staying in hotels during show rehearsals, that it would be bad luck to return to a theatre I knew but stay in a place I didn't. I was so relieved when he agreed. He explained that the current tenant was requesting a fee that amounted to ransom, but she'd stay with family with while I used the space. It would just be me and my ghosts. I paid the fee without even thinking about it.

And now I was here.

The last place I'd seen her outside of a hospital bed.

It was like there was the Before Mom—the Mom I knew was capable of anything, who raised me with stable, consistent love and joy by herself in an ever-changing city. And there was the After Mom—the woman who barely had the energy for the books she loved, for a full conversation, for anything more than trashy television while she held my hand, skin papery and cool.

Now she was gone, and something unfinished pulled on my soul. Something that demanded I spend time where everything had started.

That was why I took a low-paying theatre gig in San Francisco after I'd cleared box office records. That was why I felt simultaneously nervous and thrilled to be back in my home city. That was why, fingering the dusty edge of the blind, I couldn't bring myself to take everything in all at once.

Because I knew this was going to hurt. I knew the thing pulling on my soul was more than reconnecting with my art.

I was reconnecting with myself, putting back together the split memories into something unified and whole. Complete.

A trilling meow came from the bedroom around the corner. Sergeant Pepper leaped from the end of the bed and trotted to me in the living room, streaking my pants with long white fur, his clear blue eyes looking up at me.

"You made it," I said, bending down to scratch under his chin. He meowed in response before biting my finger. He trotted over to the kitchen and sat down with a heavy thud.

My willingness to immediately feed Sgt. Pepper was probably why he made so much noise when he sat down, but life was short for a cat. They should be as happy as possible along the way.

Finally, I found the guts to switch on the kitchen light. It was identical to how I remembered it—same ancient appliances, plastic peeling on every corner. Why would a landlord bother upgrading when they could charge a new tenant whatever they wanted after Mom moved to LA with me?

"Typical," I muttered. Jess left cat food cans neatly stacked on the counter. I set one out for Sgt. Pepper and looked around the rest of the kitchen. The fridge had a modest assortment of fruits and veggies, a six pack of Modelo, and a couple bottles of basic condiments. Setting my Frankie's leftovers on the shelf, I recognized the neon-orange price tag on the beers. It came from the corner store downstairs. I wondered if Mr. Mercedes was still behind the counter, shouting at the radio that broadcast soccer games in rapid-fire Spanish.

Probably not. No one else around here remained, I doubted the corner store owner had survived.

I cracked a beer, the sound ringing through the silent apartment as I settled in the living room. I pulled one of the blinds and watched the light flash across the wall, revealing a thick-framed mirror that ran the length of the sofa. The furniture was comfortable, if a little well-loved with frayed stitching and a few stains. I caught my own reflection before sitting down across from the TV on the opposite wall.

The same bright blue eyes I'd always had stared back at me, but that felt like the only part of me that was the same since the last time I'd stood in that very spot. My sandy blonde hair came from a bottle and was carefully applied by an expert stylist every few weeks. The sharp cut of my jaw was the result of strict dieting and even stricter workout routines. The stubble that dappled across it was a PR suggestion—it hid the small scar that slashed across my chin, the result of a playground fight when I was younger.

I sat down with a heavy sigh and clicked on the TV, flipping through a few useless channels before I turned it back off. There were no books on any of the shelves, and I puzzled over that for as long as it took me to finish the beer.

Was this a TV-only household?

I made a mental note to pick up my favorite paperbacks. If I was the only one who read them, it didn't matter. An apartment needed books like a plant needed water. Mom would've insisted.

Sgt. Pepper trotted over and settled in my lap. I let the sun warm us both and slowly I felt my eyes grow heavier and heavier.

When I woke, the sky was dark, and there was a stiff crick in my neck. Sgt. Pepper was purring like a machine, and he protested as I shifted my legs, groaning at the pins and needles that flared to life.

My stomach growled, and I wandered back into the kitchen, ignoring the fresh produce in favor of my Frankie's. But when I opened the box, I let out an anguished sigh. There was no extra BBQ sauce. Now a delicious pile of smoked meats were missing their perfectly sweet tang.

I grabbed my jacket and keys, deciding to check the corner store. Mr. Mercedes wouldn't be there, but BBQ sauce would.

Downstairs and around the far corner, I felt my chest clench at the sight of the same flickering neon sign in the window, the P blinking in and out against the steady hum of the O EN. I followed the familiar hand-painted vegetables and snacks dancing across the frame of the sunny yellow building.

Okay, so some things had stayed the same, but I couldn't get my hopes up. I braced myself for things to be different—different shelving, different products, different clerk behind the bulletproof glass. But somehow the corner store was the one place in San Francisco that hadn't been radically changed by the onslaught of tech workers. The tile was still chipped and yellow, exacerbated by the overhead lighting. A wall of fridges was at the back, and I didn't bother fighting off the munchy urges as I made my way through the aisles. By the time I'd found a bottle of BBQ sauce, I had my hands full of M&Ms, Snickers, and Reese's.

And then:

"Oye, ¿no te acuerdas de Ricardo Peláez? Es el delantero mas subestimado de la historia!" My heart soared when I recognized Mr. Mercedes behind the counter, talking to a woman with gorgeous black curls in Spanish. The two were laughing as she took a small paper bag off the counter, tucking it under her arm.

"Hi Sarah!" *God, I sound like a nerd.* I couldn't help my enthusiasm. I felt like the new kid at school who found one person to sit with at lunch.

She turned, the laughter sliding off her face as she recognized me. Was it protection I sensed from her as she looked me up and down, gaze snagging on the six candy bars in my arms?

"You're really on vacation up here, huh?" She asked, nodding to the sugar overload I was hoarding.

"Gotta get it while I can," I said. I stepped forward, brushing her soft shoulder as I set my bounty on the counter.

"Christopher?" Mr. Mercedes was an older Latino man with a shiny bald head and eyes that crinkled like waves on the shore when he smiled.

I waved, suddenly shy. "Hi, Mr. Mercedes."

He let out a long stream of Spanish that my 101 skills couldn't catch, coming around the counter with open arms. He engulfed me in a spine-crushing hug, and I let myself feel firmly held for a moment. We did the manly back-patting thing—it felt necessary after a moment like that—and he stepped away, still squeezing my shoulders with both hands.

"It is wonderful to see you again," he said, switching to English. "We miss you and your mother all the time."

"It's good to be back," I said, trying not to wince at the mention of Mom, trying not to let Sarah catch me checking to see if she reacted to the mention at all. Why did I care?

"How long are you in town?" Mr. Mercedes asked. "Just passing through?"

"Ten weeks," Sarah answered for me, chiming in from where she was pressed against the candy shelves, watching in utter confusion.

Mr. Mercedes asked her something in Spanish, his bushy brows furrowed as he listened to her response. I caught "dinner," "sweets," and "sick." Then he turned to me.

"A play," he said, nodding slowly in approval. "Very good. It's where you should be."

I suddenly needed to be out of that corner store, even if it meant returning to the dark, empty apartment upstairs. I didn't belong here—couldn't belong here—without Mom. This all felt tilted, twisted.

Wrong.

"Thanks, Mr. Mercedes," I said, shifting my weight from one foot to the other. "I'll be sure to come by for a longer visit, but it's been a really long day..." I nodded to the candy.

"For you, free," he said, waving at my load of candy and BBQ sauce. "A welcome home gift from me."

I thanked him, embarrassed, and stumbled back out onto the street, leaving the crushing familiarity behind.

"You okay?" Sarah asked from behind me, and I nearly leapt out of my skin.

"Where'd you learn to speak Spanish?" I asked, ignoring her.

"I'm Mexican," she said brusquely. "Answer the question."

"I'm fine," I sighed out. "Thanks."

"You don't look fine," she continued. I turned to see her staring at me, face pulled down with concern.

"It's nothing," I said.

"Alan will hang me from the rafters if he finds out I let you eat BBQ candy for dinner," she said, nodding at my bounty. "Come on, it's my job to make your first week easy." She nodded down the street and gestured with her free hand for me to follow.

I stuffed the candy into my jacket pockets, pulling out my baseball cap for space and privacy--I'd left the sunglasses on the kitchen counter. Sarah led me into a nearby restaurant, brightly lit with red walls and wobbly brown tables.

She sat in the far corner and gestured to the seat across from her.

"This is my favorite Chinese spot in the whole city," she said, leaning in conspiratorially. "I promise you won't go home hungry."

"My pants aren't going to fit when I leave," I said, looking over the menu.

"Mr. Mercedes said you're too skinny," she said, looking back at the menu.

"Is that what he said to you?"

"Actually he said, 'Ten weeks? And candy for dinner? Is he sick?' But I thought that might be rude to tell you straight."

I laughed, feeling the tension in my shoulders dissolve. "And yet, here we are."

"You asked."

After a few moments in silence where I tried to be interested in the menu, Sarah waved over the waitress. She pointed to a few items on the menu and ordered a Coke for herself.

"I'll have the same," I said, handing back the menu to the waitress and thanking her.

"Didn't take you for that much of a tofu guy," she said, leaning her chin in her hands. Her cheeks fit within her fingers perfectly, and my palms itched to see if they'd fit mine the same way.

"When in Rome," I said, shrugging. "I didn't want to maybe offend the vegetarian at the table."

She rolled her eyes—something I seemed to inspire a lot despite my best efforts with her.

"I'm not vegetarian, I'm just broke," she said. "Meat costs money."

My jaw dropped.

"Sarah, you're eating with a literal movie star, you can order chicken," I said. The tense moment at the staff fridge came clattering back into my memory. *Of course,* I came home and immediately forgot I was in an entirely different tax bracket than any of my new coworkers. Regret and embarrassment shot through me, pinning me in place.

"Absolutely not," she said, sitting straighter. "My invite, my treat. I would never assume--"

"Please," I said, leaning forward on the table dramatically and clasping my hands together. "Please, Sarah, let me pay for dinner." *Please let me try again. Please don't think I'm always so ignorant.*

"You don't have to do that," she said. She looked as if I'd backed her into a corner. I half expected her hackles to rise.

"You make coffee, I'll buy dinner," I said. In a desperate pitch to show I meant no harm, I laid my head down on the table, throwing my hands in the air as if I were pleading with an emperor for mercy. "Let me do this."

I heard a sigh and the tell-tale rustling of the menu's laminated pages.

"Fine," she said. When I sat up, there was a small smile on her face and a fresh light in her eyes. Her shoulders sat softer than they had before. I made a note to expressly offer to buy whenever we went out from now on.

Assuming there would be more outings.

This *was* an outing, right? Or was it something else?

"What do you usually like?" She asked, looking at me over the top of the menu, and I had to cover for the fact that my mind had been trying to turn this into a date.

"Whatever the lady recommends," I said. "You know this place better than I do. So long as you don't hold back. Tonight, we feast."

Sarah considered me for a minute, full lips pursed, brown eyes thoughtful.

"Just tonight," she said. "It's your first night back. You should celebrate."

"I should," I agreed.

She nodded once, as if reassuring herself of something, then waved at the waitress a second time. She ordered a few more dishes, flipping through multiple pages to point at different things. By the time she was done, our first plate arrived.

The shining green beans were crisped to perfection and perfectly spiced with just enough heat to tingle my mouth. They smelled incredible.

"Thank you," Sarah said, picking up her chopsticks and digging in. "For treating me."

"Thank you for bringing me here," I said, adding more green beans to my plate. We chewed in silence for a few blissful moments, savoring the dish before it would likely be eclipsed by the next.

"How long has it been since you were back?" Sarah finally asked as the waitress brought a new plate, this one heaped with steaming tofu and mushrooms, baby bok choy a shock of green in the brown.

I paused, the question hitting something sensitive in my gut.

"Ten years," I said.

"Has the Captain Arrow Star franchise been running that long?"

"No," I said, looking down at my plate.

"Good, cause I was about to feel way old," she said, laughing. Her joy was like waves on the shore, beckoning me in. I felt a grin spreading across my face of its own accord. "It's gotta be weird being back. The city's very different from what it was ten years ago."

"Yeah, it is." It was weird. It was different. I took in the contented curve of her mouth as she closed her eyes to savor a bite. "But it's not bad."

I loaded my plate with the tofu mixture, practically drooling at the wafting garlic.

"Have you always lived in the city?" I asked.

She shook her head, expertly scooping a floppy piece of tofu with her chopsticks.

"I'm from Concord," she said. "But we used to come into the city all the time, and I've always loved it. When I got picked for the housing lottery and landed so close to the theatre, I cried for like a week straight. Being here is a dream."

"Wait, you were commuting?" Concord was several hours East if traffic had anything to say about it. And if she took the BART that meant *at least* an hour each way, chugging along on the train's raised tracks that let it avoid the standstill of Bay Area traffic.

She nodded, adding extra chili oil to the remaining bok choy on her plate and eating in silence.

"That's rough," I said, unsure what else to say to break the tension. She'd suddenly clammed up, and I wondered if I'd offended her yet again.

"I managed," she said simply. We were rescued by the arrival of several dishes, including smoked duck, crispy chicken with bright spices sprinkled across the top, and—

"Are those feet?" I asked, peering at the third dish the waitress had deposited.

"The best in the city, if you're not too chicken," Sarah giggled at her own pun, coming back to herself and the food. She snapped her chopsticks together in anticipation.

"I'll try anything once." We each grabbed a foot and touched them together across the table in a sort of cheers.

The sauce was tangy and sweet with a low heat, but the texture threw me—at once soft and chewy. And there was something else...

"Don't swallow the bone," Sarah said, smiling at me like I was a confused toddler. I spit the small, hard piece out onto my plate before going back for another bite. By the time I'd finished my first foot, Sarah had moved on to the smoked duck.

"Seems like you're a foodie," she said. "What's that like in Los Angeles?"

"Miserable," I said. "World-class restaurants on every corner, and I can't eat any of it because I'm always working—training for one movie or another so I'm on a strict diet. Plain fish and asparagus or boiled chicken and egg whites."

She made a face, scooping a generous helping of duck onto my plate.

"That sounds horrible. Why do you do that to yourself?"

"Probably the same reason you commuted from Concord."

Sarah rolled her eyes.

"I didn't have a choice. I *had* to commute. You *choose* to eat like an uninspired caveman."

"I meant that you do what you have to in pursuit of your art," I said.

"I'm a PA, it's not exactly art," she said. But there was something about the set of her shoulders, the way she spoke, that told me she didn't believe that.

"Supporting the smooth execution of art counts as art in its own right," I said.

"I bet you're everyone's favorite on set."

"I can't always tell when you're being sarcastic." I watched her long lashes fold as she looked down at her plate.

"Sorry," she said. "It's just that, I didn't exactly want to be a PA."

My whole body stilled as I waited for her to continue. I worried if I so much as twitched a pinky wrong, she'd shut down again.

"It's stupid," she said, sighing and shaking her head. "And it doesn't matter." She looked back up, face breaking into a genuine smile as the waitress returned with our final dish.

"Don't people usually eat egg rolls first?" I asked.

Sarah's whole face was flush with joy, and I watched, riveted, as she delicately broke a roll in half, letting the steam waft out.

"They're the perfect last little bit," she said. "You're mostly full, but not quite satiated. Something is missing. You need that last little bit of crunch to really feel fulfilled. And an egg roll fits perfectly in that space—it's not too much, it's not too little."

She dipped one half into the small tray of spicy mustard and crunched happily. I watched the joy spread across her face, her eyes crinkled shut, her shoulders dropped down. It looked like she was experiencing exactly what she described—that she was finding her perfect, satisfying fit in that moment.

Some part of me, low and hot, wanted to be that fit.

"Will you tell me what you want to be?" I asked, barely realizing I'd asked the question out loud.

Sarah's eyes popped open in shock, and she stared at me as she swallowed.

"What?"

"Most people in your position would've opened with their ambitions," I said, words coming faster than I could control. Why was watching a girl eat an egg roll turning me on? "They've got one-on-one time with a movie star who could hook up—hook *them* up."

Get it together, Chris.

"That's not what—"

"I know," I said, cutting her off. "I know that's not what you were trying to do just now, but I feel it's only fair to offer then. Tell me what you want to be doing. I'll see what I can do to help you."

Sarah stared at me for a moment, as if I'd just offered to behead her favorite family member, and then turned, with a ricochet of curls, and asked the waitress for the check.

"Sarah—"

"No," she said, her voice brokering no argument. "I have a great job, and I live in a great apartment, and I don't *need* anything from anyone."

The waitress brought the check and as I reached for my wallet, Sarah was already standing, her paper bag from the corner store under her arm.

"Thank you for dinner," she said curtly, turning on her heel and nearly sprinting from the restaurant.

All I could do was watch her go.

SARAH

I let the door thud shut behind me and I leaned against it, breathing deep in my empty apartment. I'd left the lights on, expecting to be back in a few minutes and not the hour or so I'd spent with Chris. I could hear Amá yelling at me about wasting the electricity.

The floor lamps scattered around the living room were glowing over my abused furniture—the sofa, coffee table, and various plant stands I'd rescued from the curb, each nicked, scratched, and dented in their former-trash-heap glory. The plants themselves were cuttings from Angie who insisted even I couldn't kill a snake plant, their brown edges begging otherwise. The far wall was plastered in show posters, each and every one I'd worked on.

Angie called it my trophy wall.

The kitchen had a short breakfast bar separating the peeling linoleum from the threadbare carpet. Three cabinets hung precariously next to the fridge, barely a safe distance from my electric stove and tiny sink. Most of my food was crammed into extra bookshelves and rolling carts that I'd gathered from Facebook marketplace across the city like an interior decorator for a raccoon.

Down the dimly lit hall, covered in playbills and more show posters, was the split bathroom, the shower in one closet, the toilet and sink in another. Finally, at the end, was my miniscule bedroom, barely bigger than the double mattress flung onto the floor. I'd lined the walls with pillows and cushions, tacking clearance rack tulle to the ceiling to give it a dreamy, Moroccan vibe.

And that was it—cluttered, broken, and perfect because it was mine.

I let out one long exhale, whispering to myself, "You are so stupid."

I shoved the Cokes in the fridge, butting up against the various Tupperware of rice and beans.

Of course he was just being nice. He was a nice guy despite being a super famous actor. He'd offered to help me—specifically because I *hadn't* tried to get anything out of him like everyone else, and, in return, I'd told him exactly where he could shove it.

It wasn't about pride, despite how defensive I'd been.

I couldn't keep staring at my fridge, so I leaned across the kitchen counter to stare out the window instead, watching the flickering lights in the building across the street. People were watching TV, playing video games, making dinner, all in a perfectly contained little box I could watch from my kitchen.

Anxiety raised ghosts in my periphery again, flashing images from my past that wouldn't let me live the rest of my life in peace. Stuff like this always made the bad memories start to swallow me.

I was too scared to take the audition with Alan—he'd even offered it, after all Angie's insisting. I hadn't told Angie I turned it down, just that it wasn't happening. I was too scared to accept help from Chris—whatever that even meant.

Because I was too scared to chase what I truly wanted.

Ever since I was sixteen.

Back then, I spent every free moment in the choir room at school, practicing, hanging out with my friends, and taking extra lessons from the choir director after hours. Back then, I was fearless.

And stupid.

I thought it was normal for a teacher to pay me that much attention compared to the others. I thought it was okay for us to spend hours together in a closed room after everyone else had gone for the day. I thought we weren't doing anything but studying music together until he squeezed my knee one night when we were sitting side by side on the piano bench.

I froze. I didn't know what to do. He leaned in closer to me—closer than he'd ever been to listen, correct, listen again. If the janitor hadn't knocked to see about emptying the trash, prompting me to leap up and sprint from the room, I don't know what could've happened to me.

Then the rumors started.

Apparently, someone "saw" me hook up with the choir director. That was why I had the lead solo in the spring show. That was why I was always getting asked to demonstrate in class. Not because I had any talent or skill.

Because I was a slut.

I blamed myself. I assumed my teachers were in on the rumor as well, and God knows I couldn't bother Amá or Apá with my high school problems—not with Papi's work schedule keeping him all hours and Mami pulling doubles any chance she had. My friends abandoned me, no one else would even talk to me, and I turned into myself, clinging to whatever music I still had under the too-watchful eyes of the choir director.

It only got worse when he took my solo and gave it to another student. He said my failure to show for private lessons meant I wasn't ready.

I didn't know I could've reported him. I didn't know what he was doing was wrong.

All I knew was singing attracted punishment, so it was best if I stayed away from it.

Even with a few free therapy calls through my insurance and a lot of drunk conversations with Angie, 10 years later I still felt all the old fears rise at the very mention of singing in front of anyone. I was still terrified I'd be told I didn't deserve it, that I wasn't good enough, that I'd done something *extra* to get a slot I didn't deserve.

And yet, singing was the only thing that made all those old ghosts disappear.

Checking the time on my phone, I decided it wasn't too late to be *that* neighbor for 3 minutes and 49 seconds. I turned on my TV, an antiquated behemoth with several adapters along the back to allow for my streaming stick. I had to wait for the screen to warm up. I tapped my phone a few times to connect to the speakers. I rounded the kitchen counter, coming to stand square with the screen.

I closed my eyes and let the recorded orchestra wash over me, counting under my breath to the opening phrase.

The first line of the song pressed out from between my lips. I pushed with my lungs to set the next line free. Slowly, I slipped into the song and forgot that anyone might hear me, following the dramatic expressions of the singer.

I felt my heart spin, felt my shoulders drop, felt my gut untangle itself. I imagined myself on the stage I had crossed so many hundreds of times. This time, the lights were on me, the seats were filled.

I imagined Chris in the front row, awed by the final crescendo as I matched every note with the singer in the recording.

And then it was over, leaving me shaking and a little heartbroken in my living room. The orchestra faded out and in the few moments of silence before the song began again on autoplay, I heard a soft knock on my door. I turned the TV off and braced myself before opening the door.

"I'm so sorry, I—"

Chris stood there, staring, blue eyes wide beneath his perfect floppy hair. We stood in silence. Had he heard me? He had to have heard me. How long had he been standing there?

"I brought you leftovers," he said, voice barely more than a whisper. He held up a plastic takeout bag that looked like it was already leaking.

I took it, silently, and let the door swing shut.

When the latch clicked, I swore under my breath.

This was going to make work so *weird* in the morning.

I met Chris in the hall the next morning, fully prepared to ignore that he'd probably heard me singing my heart out at full volume.

I would *not* be explaining myself, no matter how gentle his smile or how welcoming his presence. I would shove coffee in his hand and guide the conversation away far, far away from singing.

No one would be able to say I'd done anything other than give a movie star a cup of coffee out of kindness from exactly three feet away.

Chris was freshly showered, bright-eyed and bushy tailed, ready for the world. I felt like I was going to murder the next creature that walked in front of me. Despite what I'd promised myself, I had *not* woken up early enough to do my makeup, and I was ruffled from having tossed and turned all night.

He *heard* me. No one had ever heard me sing like that. At karaoke sometimes or when goofing off at cast parties—but never like *that*. Never when I meant it.

And I always meant "Back to Before."

"Ready?" I asked, finding a smile somewhere and shoving it on my face.

He rubbed his hands together greedily and gave me an evil smile.

"Coffee, coffee, coffee," he said in a cartoonish voice.

I cocked my head, a giggle tearing free in surprise.

"It's nothing fancy," I said. My faded travel mug looked especially shabby in his well-manicured hand.

He took a sip, closing his eyes, and let out a satisfied sigh.

"I can taste the barely restrained annoyance," he said with a wink.

I laughed, feeling it bounce in the hall around us, hesitating as the joy landed back in my chest despite my best efforts to squash it. He smelled just as good as yesterday, and I had to scoot against the wall to get past him to the stairs.

"Come on, you weirdo," I called over my shoulder.

"So, you *don't* hate me?" he asked, catching up with me.

"I hate anyone who asks for coffee like that this early in the day."

"You don't know Dick Dastardly?"

"Was I supposed to get that from your impression?"

"You *wound* me, fair lady," he pretended to fall back on the stair landing, clutching his heart. "I am a trained professional, surely my Dastardly is up to par."

I shrugged. "I think Hollywood might be babying you a little."

"Does that mean I'm *not* the sexiest man alive?"

I sucked air through my teeth, pretending I was breaking bad news.

We made the short walk to the theatre laughing about old-school cartoons and trying to do our best impressions. My Fred Flintstone made him nearly trip in the street, and it turns out he could do the entire line-up for Wacky Races.

Fog rolled in from the water, the morning sun doing its best to wink through in bright patches of blue before they were submerged in grey. I was thrilled that he wasn't asking about the singing—and, okay, also that a hot movie star was paying such close attention to me. Chris meant it when he made eye contact, when he leaned in, when he laughed at a joke, or his face dropped in sympathy.

He was honest. And entirely himself, despite the Hollywood wrapping he seemed to be slowly shedding.

It wasn't until we were nearly there, passing the private school across the street, that he said the thing I'd been dreading for more than twelve hours.

"So, I didn't know you could sing like that."

"Like what?" I asked, not doing a very good job of playing dumb.

"Like you're an aristocratic mother at the turn of the century lamenting the massive changes she sees coming."

"Please, don't make a big deal out of it," I said, slamming the crosswalk button harder than I meant to.

"I won't if you don't want me to, but Sarah, you have real talent," he said. I wanted it to be Hollywood schmoozing. I wanted it to be flirting. I wanted it to be anything but the incredibly genuine and earnest praise he was offering me, all soft smiles and honest eyes. "What are you doing in the wings?"

The light changed, and I charged out into the street, panic biting at every step.

"Okay, okay, you don't have to tell me," Chris said, jogging to catch up with me, expertly dodging street debris and cracks in the sidewalk. "But I am going to leave this offer on the table indefinitely."

He stopped, blocking my path and forcing me to relent my one-woman charge to the theatre. He didn't touch me, but I felt held in place by his clear gaze.

"You ever want to sing," he said. "In *any* capacity. For any reason. Tell me. And if you don't want help making it happen, then at least tell me when and where so I can be there to hear you again."

The street was too loud, my chest was too tight, Chris was too close to be saying things like that. My skin was crawling with a thousand invisible bugs, and I needed to stomp them to death. I swiveled my gaze, frantically checking for any cast or crew members.

"I'm not that good," I said shaking my head, desperate for a piece of reality to anchor me. "You're spending too much time around professional lip syncers."

"Sarah," and this time he did touch me, reaching a single gentle hand and resting it on my shoulder. His hand was warm even through my jacket, and it cupped the top of my shoulder perfectly. The bugs stopped, my breath hitched, the street fell silent. "You have a beautiful voice, and you use it like an expert. I'd be stupid to miss a chance to hear you again like I did last night."

"Through a wall?" I asked. I resisted the urge to rub myself under his hand like a hungry cat. Instead, I reached up and touched the tip of his fingers, reassuring myself that he was here, and this was real, in a moment that was threatening to disassociate out from under me.

"If through a wall is the only way to hear you, then I'll be pressed against every wall in the city for the rest of my life."

He meant it, too. I could see it in his face.

Before I could process my stomach swooping and my pulse throbbing in places it shouldn't, a shrill voice interrupted from behind me.

"Oh my god, are you Chris Oldfelds?" A rail-thin teenager with bottle-blonde hair and the signature San Francisco Academy uniform screamed in my ear. Her classmates were crossing the street behind her, and I could see in my periphery that more were coming.

"Good morning," Chris smiled wide and welcoming, but something about it seemed strange. The sincere person who'd just stopped me dead in my tracks suddenly vanished behind glittering teeth and rippling abs.

"Oh my god you *are! You're him!*" She screamed again and waved wildly to her friends.

I caught Chris' eye and mouthed "okay?"

He nodded, leaning over to whisper from the corner of his mouth, "Just don't leave me."

I stayed, watching as Chris patiently signed notebooks and took endless selfies until I was sure half of the Academy student body had bee-lined straight for him.

"Alright, everybody," I threw my hands in the air, waving my now empty coffee cup like a banner. It had been nearly an hour, and we'd drastically cut into Chris' appointment with the costume department. Marisol was going to be furious. "That's it for Mr. Oldfelds, he's got rehearsals to get to. Contemporary American Theatre offers student discounts, and his show opens in October."

I shouldered my way through the tiny mob and looped an arm through Chris', pulling him back up the street toward the theatre.

"Thank you!" he called out, nearly tripping on himself to wave goodbye.

"They were going to take you to fourth period with them," I said. My brain told me to unhook myself from his side, but when he didn't move to break apart either, I decided to stay. It was comfortable, walking arm in arm like this.

Chris ran a hand over his face and sighed. "They keep me working, but it can be a lot some days." He gestured with his coffee cup. "This is cold now."

"We can get you a new coffee, but not a new body. Come on, Marisol is gonna murder us both," I said. We walked the rest of the way in silence, all the things he'd said before the teenie boppers fell upon him were still bouncing through my mind. One phrase kept ricocheting, pinging off my pounding heart and ribs.

"...for the rest of my life."

I untangled myself from our locked arms as we neared the theatre, shoving away the pang of disappointment that accompanied it. The side entrance was unlocked this time—no interference from Angie—and I said goodbye to Chris at the door to the costume department. Before I could get too far down the hall, he called after me, door cracked open.

"Think about it? What I said earlier?"

I could only nod, ducking into the wings before anyone heard or saw.

"You better tell me everything." I shrieked at Angie's surprise appearance. In the low house lights, her black jeans, dark t-shirt, and endless waves of dark hair nearly made her blend in with the curtains, leaving just her bobbing, mischievous face.

"Did we wake up feeling like the Cheshire?" I asked, gesturing at her getup. She stepped forward, the rest of her materializing from the drapery.

"If you'd just tell me things, I wouldn't have to camouflage," she said.

"What are you talking about?"

"I talked to Alan," she said, crossing her arms. I turned and headed toward the shelves near the back door where we kept our bags and coats.

"Why?" I asked, again realizing how bad I was at playing stupid.

"He said he offered you the audition when I told him how talented you were," she said. "He said you *turned it down*."

"So?" I asked, ripping my bag open and pulling out my trusty three-ring binder.

"'*So?*' Sarah, why are you lying to me about this?"

"Ang, please, I tried to tell you I didn't want to do it, and you didn't listen," I said, shoving my bag onto the shelf with more force than was necessary. "I told you it was my chance to take or not."

"I didn't think you'd actually reject the whole thing entirely."

"Well," I turned to see Angie glowering at me. "Now you know I would."

We glared at each other in silence for a moment before Angie tilted her chin up at me defiantly.

"Tell him you changed your mind," she said.

"Let it go, Angie." I closed my eyes against her challenging stare.

Between last night and now, it was too much. People were being so nice to me, and it felt like a trap—a trap I hadn't escaped before, how could I possibly do it again? My eyes grew hot, and I feared the tears that threatened to leak out. If I cried at work I'd have to retire before I even got started. I'd never be able to live with myself.

"Please, Sarah, at least try," she said, stepping forward and taking one hand in hers with a soft squeeze. "If you totally bomb no one will ever know, and I'll shut up about it for the rest of our lives."

"Our lives? Are you proposing?" I teased, opening my eyes and swiping at them with the back of my free hand. I had to break the tension. I had to smother her kindness—or I *would* cry, and I wasn't ready for early bird specials just yet. Angie rolled her eyes and kissed me on the cheek.

"You should be so lucky," she said. "But don't change the subject."

"Let me think about it, okay?" I sighed, feeling the tension slide away, the drained exhaustion of an emotional whirlwind taking its place.

"I need to know by Friday," she said. "Marisol wants to do karaoke after rehearsal, and we all know you won't say no. I'll invite Alan—"

"You wouldn't."

"—if you don't at least think about it," she finished, holding her hands up for peace. "Geez, Sarah, I'm not evil, I'm just meddling."

"Tell me again how those are different?"

She winked again, twirling on her heel in a flare of jet-black hair.

I rolled my eyes, following her to where the rest of the crew was gathering for the weekly staff meeting.

My best friend was going to kill me with her good intentions.

Chris

The day passed in a blur and through all the fittings, blockings, and read-throughs, I found myself constantly looking for a head of bouncing black curls. I couldn't stop thinking about her powerful, emotive voice that stopped me in my tracks even through a closed door.

San Francisco apartment walls weren't known for being sound-proof, but I still desperately wanted to hear Sarah sing without barriers.

What was she so afraid of?

And how could I get her to open up without scaring her off?

As the rest of the cast wrapped for the day, I looked around, yet again, for Sarah. I hadn't seen her all day, and I couldn't remember enough about theatre life to know if that meant she was avoiding me or not.

"Chris, you want to join us?" Nicole asked.

"Sorry, join what?" I hadn't been listening while I was looking for Sarah.

"Dinner," she said, wrapping a silk scarf around her neck. "We're going up the street together. Why don't you come?"

I didn't want to. I wanted to walk home with Sarah and hear about her day. I wanted to know where she'd been. I wanted to ask for her Fred Flintstone impression again, just to watch the way her eyes crinkled when she laughed. I felt like a kid with a crush, waiting by a girl's locker even though the bell rang hours ago.

"Maybe another time," Nicole said after I failed to answer. She gave me a friendly smile and readjusted her bag.

"No, no, I'll come," I said, finally. I gave the theatre one last scan before following Nicole out into the lobby.

You're just lonely, I thought to myself, trying to shake the sense that I was betraying Sarah by not waiting.

Nicole and I walked a few paces behind the other actors, making small talk. She was originally from Ohio, and she had a serious boyfriend who worked in tech doing something I didn't fully understand. She had a warm presence, and I soon found myself relaxing into the comfort of our conversation.

The ten of us found space in the back of a Vietnamese restaurant, ordering enough pho and beer to feed an army. I listened as the others shared inside jokes, teased one another, and used Shakespeare lines to make puns about the Giants. Nicole helped translate the comradery, letting me in on the jokes and holding the door open for me into their friendship.

"So, did you ask her yet?" A timid, petite blonde woman, Anna, asked the brooding hipster sitting across from her.

"No, I thought about it, and it feels...wrong," the hipster answered. "Why?"

"It's all a little upstairs-downstairs, ya know?"

"What do you mean?" I asked. The hipster looked at me, pushing dark hair out of his eyes. I was pretty sure his name was Leon. He'd given me a sneer when I first joined rehearsals yesterday, and I'd ignored it. I wondered if his face just looked like that.

"You probably know better than the rest of us," he said, pausing to take a sip of his beer. "How you can't fraternize with the crew."

"You can't?" I asked, trying to tamp down the annoyance I felt rising in my core.

"Of course," he said. "It looks bad. Paul says it gives people the wrong impression. For lack of a better way to put it, it's gauche." I didn't miss the long emphasis he put on the Artistic Director's name.

"How very *gauche* for His Royal Highness to be caught with the scullery maid." Nicole's tone was sharp, and she was giving Leon's sneer a run for his money.

"It's also a power imbalance," came a voice from the far end of the table. Heads whipped in the direction of Rebecca, an older white woman who played the visiting Countess to my and Nicole's wealthy married couple. "Dating the crew might cause friction between colleagues. And you may never know *why* that crewmember was interested in you in the first place. It's all very messy. I'm with Leon, and Paul, best to just not."

I shook my head. "You all agree with him?"

"You more than any of us should be careful, Chris," Rebecca continued. "One wrong move and that crewmember could cry 'me too!' Then you're really screwed."

"Rebecca that's gross. It puts a blight on the movement," Nicole snapped. She pushed her seat back from the table sending everyone's pho sloshing across the wobbly surface. "I've lost my appetite."

I followed her as she stormed from the restaurant, leaving the rest of the cast wiping at their laps and staring after us in shock.

"I'm so sorry," Nicole said as we rounded a corner, leaving the restaurant behind us. "I'm sorry about them, and I'm sorry for making things awkward. Those two really push my buttons."

"Which two?" I asked, matching her rage-induced quick-step.

"Rebecca and Leon," she said. "This is the third show we've done together. Each time they find something new to piss me off with. But Rebecca's really taking the cake tonight. And Leon's obviously just jealous you beat him out for the lead, even though he spends all his free time spitting in Paul's ear."

"You don't agree with them?" I asked, watching Nicole's face closely.

"*God no*," she huffed. "You want to date a crew member go for it. I prefer not to shit where I eat, but it's not because I think I'm too highbrow or 'targeted' to do it."

I laughed. "I guess it is still a job and everyone *is* coworkers. Sometimes I forget that."

"Really?" She looked surprised, delicate eyebrows arched high on her face. She'd slowed to a normal pace as we got further from the restaurant.

I shrugged. It was hard to remember that I was working when the thing I did every day brought me such unbridled joy. It didn't *feel* like work for me. Which didn't always mean it wasn't work for someone else.

Nicole stopped in front of a MUNI stop, pulling a pair of headphones from her pocket. "I'm gonna head home," she said, nodding toward the sign. "I'm sorry again but thank you for coming with us anyway."

"Next time it'll be just us two," I offered. "Or maybe we'll find a way to ditch Rebecca and Leon."

She gave me a bright smile. "I'd love that."

We waved goodnight, and I walked back to my apartment building, my head spinning in a thousand different directions.

Back at the apartment, I thought my eyes were playing tricks on me when I started the stairs only to see bobbing black curls in front of me.

"Sarah?"

She turned around, eyes wide, lips parted. Slowly, she smiled, as if unsure what the two of us were doing in the stairwell. A warm relief flooded my system.

"Fancy meeting you here," I joked, catching up with her.

"Do you come here often?" She joked back. But there was something stilted between us, a hesitancy that had grown over the course of the day.

We made it up the stairs and into the hall before I finally caved.

"I'm sorry," I said. "If I made you uncomfortable."

"You didn't," she said, shaking her head. "You made me more comfortable than stupid Angie and all her pushing."

"It's your life," I said. "And it's your voice. You decide what you're comfortable doing." My fingers twitched at my sides, aching to reach out to her. I shoved them in my pockets, gripping the liner fabric hard enough to tear.

Sarah fiddled with her keys, and I noticed a small cat keychain dangling from her ring.

"You mean it?"

My heart clenched in my chest at the tentative way she asked, at how soft her voice became in that tender moment.

"With all my being, Sarah," I said. "I've never heard anyone sing like you and that was through a wall. I can only imagine what it's like in person."

"You're not just being nice to the sad little PA?" She was staring at the cat keychain like it might start talking to her.

"Ask anyone else on the show," I said. "I haven't offered anything to anyone. Just you."

She nodded but still wouldn't look at me.

I knew I should stop standing in the hallway, that I should let her go, that we shouldn't linger here like the world's dorkiest fire hazard. But I was frozen in place, unable to tear my gaze away from her.

"Do you have a cat?" I'd struck up casual conversations with Tom Hanks and Beyonce. How was Sarah undoing me like this?

She looked at me from under her thick lashes, and my heart clenched again at the flash in her eyes.

Right. Like that.

"The keychain was a gift," she said. "Maybe someday I'll take the leap and get a cat."

"Take the leap?"

"The timing never seemed right. I work weird hours, and I'd hate for my new roommate to get lonely."

"I'll have to introduce you to Sergeant Pepper," I said.

"I know about the Beatles," she said, arching an eyebrow at me.

"He's my cat," I said. "He's kinda fat cause I overfeed him, but he's the best cat in the world."

"I don't get down to LA often," she said, returning to fidget with her keys.

"No, he's here with me," I said pointing at my door. "You could meet him right now if you wanted."

Something in Sarah's stance shifted, and she turned to put her keys in the lock, doing an expert shimmy to get the door open.

"That's alright," she said shaking her head. "I'll see you tomorrow."

"For coffee?" I asked. She hesitated before nodding.

"Your treat this time," she said. I caught a glimpse of a smile before the door closed, and I was left alone in the hall.

SARAH

A movie star just invited me into his apartment, and I turned him down. Angie would be furious.

But I couldn't do it. As gorgeous as he was, and as kind and earnest as our time together had been, he'd caught me singing and had offered to—what exactly? "Help me?"

No. I knew where that "help" led. And his dark, empty apartment held too many similarities to the choir practice room where my entire life had been tilted by a single gesture.

I felt myself pushing away from Chris—as much as I could, given we worked in a tiny theatre, and he lived across the hall from me.

I opened and closed my fridge, disappointed yet again by the stacks of beans that wouldn't somehow disappear. Then I remembered the leftovers.

I microwaved some fried rice and smoked duck, cracking open one of the Cokes I'd brought home the night before. While the food spun in the microwave, I tried to sort through the tidal wave crashing over me.

It all felt like too much. Like somehow, more than a decade later, I'd be inviting the same kind of trouble as I'd landed in at 16 simply by following a few notes on the page. It would be that locked room all over again, and every time I tried it was all I could see behind my eyes.

No. Better to stay in the wings where I was hidden and safe. No one could accuse me, sneer at me, leave me behind for doing my job in the shadows.

The microwave beeped, and I jumped despite myself. I decided it would be a self-care night. Just me, Chinese food, and some exceptionally trashy reality TV until it was time for bed.

As I clicked on the TV, flipping through the various apps connected to my streaming stick, I thought about what Angie said earlier—about taking the audition after all. I had promised to tell her before Friday or else she'd invite Alan to karaoke. God help me—that could *not* happen.

I *could* say yes. I *could* audition. Maybe it'd put all this chaos behind us. Maybe Angie would leave me alone and I could return to my wings in peace.

I settled into the couch, punching play on the remote.

This was all a problem for tomorrow. Tonight, I was done thinking about *anything* or *anyone*.

The next few days passed in a blur—set tests, construction, blocking rehearsals, and an especially frustrating day trying to source vintage wing-back chairs. The living room set we'd asked to borrow from our sister theatre in Berkeley had mysteriously gone missing. I spent the day sprinting in and out of antique shops, haggling with store owners and explaining that we were an arts non-profit not a movie production. By the time I staggered through the door, my feet hurt, and I had zero patience left.

To make matters worse, my morning walks to the theatre with Chris were stilted and polite. We talked about the fog almost every day, never delving into anything deeper than what we could see in front of us. Sometimes we walked in tense silence while I picked at the crumbling handle on my tumbler, convinced I'd never get the chance to see the earnest, smiling, real version of Chris he'd presented so readily before.

And still Friday loomed, and every time I thought about the closed room, the yellow light, the upright piano not quite in tune where I'd audition, my throat closed, my palms sweat, my head swam.

I tried repeating to myself that Alan was a trusted member of the community. Alan was a good guy. Alan was not my choir teacher, and I was not sixteen.

Nothing worked. My old fears were embedded in my skin, as much a part of me as the scar on my right wrist from a tough lesson with a table saw. I woke up sweating Thursday night, the image of my choir teacher's dusty, cracked lips looming closer and closer to me, the feeling of his hand gripping my knee so vivid I frantically scrubbed my hands down my legs to make sure I'd just been dreaming.

Then, it was Friday.

The Berkeley theatre finally found the furniture set, so I was in the wings again, set free from questing to yet another antique shop.

"So?" came Angie's voice from over my shoulder, making me jump.

"Are you *sure* you're not secretly the theatre ghost?" I asked, swatting at her. She swatted back playfully.

"I told you not to tease about that, you'll make the ghost mad," she said, putting a finger to her lips.

"Aren't you supposed to be testing pyrotechnics for the gunfire scenes?" I asked.

Angie shrugged. "They can't explode without me so why rush?"

I rolled my eyes.

"Your answer?" She asked, twirling her hips and sticking her bottom lip out at me.

"Answer to what?"

"Sarah Aguilar, don't you play dumb with me."

I sighed. "Can you give me another week?"

"No."

"You'd make a brutal loan shark."

"Answer, please."

"Angie..."

"Oh, Sarah." She put a hand on my arm, skimming down to grip my fingers. She said my name with such gentleness, such understanding. My skin lit with all those bugs, and I shook free of her hand.

"If I take the audition, will you leave me alone about ever auditioning again?" My voice was sharp and annoyed, but I felt quietly resigned. It was time to face this fear. Or to at least get Angie to leave me alone.

I'd probably bomb the audition anyway.

Angie squealed in delight, jumping in place.

I held my hand out for calm, checking to see if anyone else noticed. Angie put her hands over her mouth, nodding furiously.

"I will tell Alan I changed my mind about auditioning—"

Another shriek.

"And I will audition. But that's it! I never want to hear about it again."

Angie stuck her hand out, and I shook it like a middle-aged man concerned with appearances. Before I could let go, Angie hauled me into a massive hug. She was deceptively strong given her slight frame.

"I'm so proud of you," she whispered, and I felt my insides wiggle. The bugs crawled, my gut tightened, my eyes grew hot.

"If you make me cry at work, the deal's off."

She immediately released me, dramatically pretending to dust off my shoulders as if I'd been dragged through the dirt.

"Go blow things up," I said, swatting at her hands. "I'll find Alan."

As Angie melted back into the wings, I followed the director's booming voice to the back of House where he was talking with Dorian, our production manager.

I cleared my throat, nodding a polite hello Dorian over Alan's shoulder. If I sweat anymore, I was going to slide down the vom and into the orchestra pit. Could they hear my heart slamming in my chest?

Alan turned around, eyebrows rocketing up his forehead. I wished there was a trapdoor under me—preferably one connected to the parking lot so I could escape faster.

"Sarah, everything alright?" Alan asked as Dorian waved goodbye, giving us a semblance of privacy in a bustling theatre.

"More than alright," I said.

"How are you doing with Chris? He seems particularly fond of you," he smiled. "Thank you for putting in the extra effort to show him around."

I tucked away that comment for later inspection. My nerves couldn't handle Chris being "fond" of me on top of everything else.

"I want to talk to you about the audition for Company."

"I thought you weren't interested?" His brows knit together, and he moved to hold his ever-present folio with both hands.

"I wasn't," I said. "But…"

I let the silence hang between us, unsure how to continue.

"Now you are?" He prompted.

I nodded, relieved.

"I told you I would make time," he said. "And I meant it. But don't change your mind on me a second time."

"I won't," I said.

"What *did* change your mind?"

"I got some extra encouragement," I said.

"From a certain visiting actor?" He asked, tipping his glasses to the end of his sharp nose.

"From a meddling best friend," I said flushing to the tips of my ears. "She said she'd invite you to karaoke if I didn't audition. I think we'd both prefer that didn't happen."

Alan let out a booming laugh which shuddered into my feet. I couldn't help the grin in response.

"Yes, yes, I think we would both prefer that didn't happen."

We set a time for a few weeks after *Caught Red-Handed* opened, giving me time to prepare—and giving Alan time to clear his schedule.

"I want to be present for every audition," he said. "I remember how much work they are. I don't want to cheat you of that."

I thanked him, heading back to the wings as the actors filed onstage. I felt like I was floating, buoyed by Alan's promise—by the possibility of singing again. I'd spent so long afraid of it, I forgot how exciting it could be when it was new and fresh and only just getting prepared.

But by the time I reached the wings, the cold reality of the situation set in.

I would be in a closed room, alone, with a man I'd come to trust. And I'd be singing. Just like last time.

Cold hands gripped my heart.

"What'd he say?" Angie asked as we noted down a shift in blocking for Act Two.

"I'm doing it," I said, sounding like I was killing a man and not singing a couple stanzas.

Angie squeezed my shoulder. "Don't be nervous, Sarah, you'll crush it."

Only if I didn't get crushed first.

I couldn't think about anything else for the rest of rehearsal. I missed blocking notes, dropped my headset, and was nearly run over by set crew when they came in with the furniture from Berkeley.

"The audition is in a few weeks, not today," Angie hissed at me when I stepped on the back of her foot for the third time in a row. "Chill out."

By the time we broke for the night, I felt like every nerve in my body was rattling on a new level—as if someone had taken my dial and cranked it to eleven.

"Are you going to be okay at karaoke, or should I send you home with a bottle of wine?"

I shook my head. I needed to blow off steam, or I was going to explode.

"I'm definitely in."

"Great, Chris is coming," she threw casually over her shoulder as she walked off.

The world tilted as my fingers went numb.

"Oh my god," I whispered to myself.

"There you are!" I jolted, turning to see Chris beaming down at me, already in his jacket with his secret disguise baseball cap pushed up on his head. "Angie invited me to karaoke with you guys. I just hope my 'Wells Fargo Wagon' isn't too rusty."

I nodded dumbly.

"That's not really my go-to song," he waggled his eyebrows at me. "You're not allowed to make fun of me. It's kinda—"

"I wanted to meet your cat," I blurted out. Our last awkward interaction had been hanging over me, regardless of our painfully polite walks to coffee every morning that week. He'd taken the hint and backed off—because *of course* he had. I still wasn't sure if the cat was real, or he was using a very bad pick-up line. It didn't matter.

I hated not seeing him.

"Okay," he said, eyes never leaving my face. "You still can."

"Doors make me nervous," I said.

"Sgt. Pepper would probably demand I take it off the hinges if a door is what's keeping you from him," he said, eyes crinkling. If I stood on my tiptoes, I wondered if I could kiss his smile lines.

"Sgt. Pepper would demand it?" I asked.

"I am merely his servant. He is the king of the apartment."

I laughed, comfort stretching out across my heart and making itself at home. This was why I liked Chris. No questions, no judgements. Just his straightforward self.

I'd missed him.

The thought bloomed like a particularly confusing flower in a fast-forward garden, so that by the time Angie joined us to walk to karaoke I had already watched it take root, sprawl out, flex its petals, and put itself on full display in the sun.

And all I could think to myself was, *I really did miss him. And I don't know what that means.*

CHRIS

Sarah was laughing again—at *my* stupid jokes. Relief bloomed between us, but there was something else. Some nameless feeling growing in my chest when her brown eyes searched my face.

She'd shut me out for days and it had somehow felt like weeks. Whatever her reason, I had no choice but to wait for her to open again, offering whatever polite small talk I could tolerate on our walks to work each morning. I'd been asking her about the weather when I'd wanted to ask her about her favorite ice cream flavor, about what her parents cooked growing up, about the first time she fell and got back up again.

It was torture.

Now, enroute to karaoke with her friend Angie, hands shoved in our pockets against the cold August air, it felt like the girl I had a crush on found me in the hall.

And let's be real, this was *definitely* a crush. A big one.

Something was building between us. I could feel it. Something that seemed to have only flourished despite the emotional distance.

Loony Tune's neon sign loomed in the fog, appearing like a vision before three exhausted artists.

"What's your go-to?" I asked.

"'I Believe in a Thing Called Love,'" Angie said, sliding a glance at Sarah that had to mean something.

"'Stop, in the Name of Love,'" Sarah retorted, rolling her eyes.

"Is this some kind of code or are those actually your songs?" I asked.

"You have to get a drink and find out," Angie shrugged.

The karaoke place was set up like a vintage lounge, red velvet drapes hanging from every wall, flickering electric tea lights on every low table. It smelled like sweat and spilled vodka and was nearly empty this early in the day.

"Fanfare for the queens!" A rail-thin man yelled from behind the bar. He had a long handlebar mustache and wore a vest that would be more at home in a circus ring. "The Queens of Karaoke have returned!"

"Marcus!" Angie and Sarah cried in unison.

"You guys are like *regular* regulars." But my comment was left in the dust as the two women leapt across the bar and into a crushing hug from Marcus.

"I haven't even fired up the screens yet," Marcus said when he finally released them. "What brings you in so early?"

"It's been a long week," Angie said before pointing to me across the room. "We brought a newbie."

"He looks a lot like Chris Oldfelds."

"I get that all the time," I said, grinning.

"Will you make drinks if we kick things off?" Angie clasped her hands together and held them far from her face, whispering "please" repeatedly.

"Whatever the Queens command!" He bowed dramatically before stepping behind the bar and beginning a complicated dance with multiple different liquor bottles.

I watched as Angie and Sarah kicked into action, two practiced experts in execution on their home turf. Sarah turned equipment on and plugged in cords to speakers and screens on the stage across the bar. Angie place two microphones in their stands, clicking each on and doing a short sound check with a dirty limerick. Sarah laughed while she adjusted knobs and dials, Angie setting off into yet another verse.

I had to admit, watching them, I felt left out.

"They're something, huh?" Marcus appeared at my elbow with a pint glass cocktail, complete with skewered fruit and a brightly colored umbrella.

"I'm lucky to work with them," I said, taking the glass and sipping cautiously. It was mostly liquor with a little fruit juice. I winced. "You'll send me to bed early with these."

"Everyone needs liquid courage to get on stage," he winked, sealing for me that he really didn't know what I did for a living.

"I've got first!" Angie yelled into the microphone, inspiring another wince.

Marcus brought each of the women a drink before shooing Sarah away from the DJ booth. Angie leaned over to him and whispered something behind her hand.

The opening piano bars of "I Left My Heart in San Francisco" kicked off, and Angie began crooning in a sweet alto. Sarah came and stood next to me, sipping on her drink and swaying along.

Angie pointed to me as she continued then pointed to Sarah and motioned with her hands for us to dance.

Maybe it was the realization that I'd missed Sarah throughout the week, or the stinging way the song hit my gut, but I set my drink down and offered Sarah my hand.

She eyed it for a moment before setting her own drink down and taking it. Her hands were soft and warm in mine as I pulled her close to me. We swayed together in a loose circle as the bar around us melted away. I couldn't remember the last time my heart pounded this hard as I looked at her upturned face.

"I'm auditioning for Alan," she said. I could barely hear her over Angie's crooning, so I leaned in closer, tilting my ear to her in a way I hoped meant "I can't hear you" and not "stick your nose in my ear."

"I'm auditioning for Alan," she said again. Her warm breath grazed my ear, sending a thrill down my spine that was quickly eclipsed by joy as I realized what she'd said. My face split into a grin so big it hurt my cheeks.

"That's amazing, Sarah," I said. "Singing?"

She nodded, glancing away.

"I told him it was because Angie threatened to bring him to karaoke," she said. "But there was another reason."

Could she feel my heart slamming in my chest? Did she know how twisted my stomach was, waiting for her to speak again?

"What reason was that?"

"We better all get a turn dancing with Chris!" The voice shrieked out across the bar. Sarah practically vaulted herself away from me as her coworkers filed into the bar.

Angie hit her final notes and bowed to scattered applause. She handed the microphone to Sarah who waved it away.

"I need to drink more first," she said. Before Angie could hand it to me, I found myself snatched up by a burly guy from set crew, embraced tenderly in his large arms.

"Someone do Celine," he yelled over my shoulder. "I'm about to make a dream come true."

I laughed and let him take the lead as another crew member took the microphone and launched into a slightly off-pitch rendition of "My Heart Will Go On."

The night continued this way, with Sarah disappearing and my own drink melting in a corner somewhere as crew member after crew member claimed a slow dance with me.

Angie finally took the microphone back, announcing that "slow dancing hour was closed" before kicking off a classic Ramones hit.

By now the bar was packed, mostly with people from the theatre, drinking, laughing, talking loudly over the music. I searched the room for Sarah, finally finding her at the bar laughing at something Marcus said. Her curls bounced as she threw her head back, and I felt a pang of jealousy. There was no hesitation with Marcus, just true, effortless Sarah beaming at him from across the top of her glass.

"I'll have what she's having," I said, sitting down next to her at the bar. I hated the line as it fell flat, practically thudding onto the sticky wood surface.

Marcus squinted at me before arching his eyebrows at Sarah.

"Really?" he said. Sarah blushed, the heat creeping down her neck.

"Don't be mean, Marcus, please," she said.

"You're lucky you're so hot," he said, wagging a finger at me.

"If I had a nickel for every time I heard that," I said.

"You'd be richer than you are now?" Sarah teased. I stuck my tongue out at her. Marcus slid a drink to me, and I took a sip, immediately shuddering.

"What *is* this?"

"Long Island Ice Tea with coffee instead of tea," she said, sipping nonchalantly.

"It is disgusting," I said, taking another sip and bracing myself against the bar.

"Easy there, buddy, it's my signature," she said, shooting me a mock glare.

"You need a different signature," I laughed.

We watched Angie finish her Ramones song and in the lull between performances, I drummed my fingers on the bar, trying to fill the silence.

"You're really going to audition?" I asked. I thought for the millionth time about her voice through the door. "Is it closed?"

"What do you mean?" She cocked her head at me, throwing her curls to one side. The lights from the karaoke stage flashed across her face. My heart squeezed and I felt a little light-headed.

"Is it a closed audition or are people allowed to watch?"

"People watch auditions?" Her jaw dropped open, her eyes growing wide.

"I mean, not usually," I said. "But they could. If you'd let them."

Something strange crossed her face as she looked down at her shoes for a moment.

"I hadn't thought about it," she said, looking back up at me with a renewed energy. "But yes, I think people will be allowed to watch."

"Then I'll be there," I said. "And I bet Angie will be too."

Suddenly, her arms were around me, and I was enveloped in her smell, all citrus shampoo and liquored coffee. I had the sense to automatically wrap my arms around her, returning the hug, and something in my core lit on fire at the sensation of her pressed so closely to me.

"Thank you," she said, inches from my face, eyes glowing in the stage lights. "You have no idea...just thank you."

"Calling Sarah to the stage, Miss Sarah Aguilar," Angie had taken the mic again and shooed someone else away. "It's been a million years, get up here girl."

Sarah pulled away as every head in the room whipped around. People whistled and cheered as she made her way to the stage.

"The usual?" Angie asked into the mic as she handed it to Sarah, who only nodded.

As Angie queued the song, ignoring Marcus' shouts that he'd be right there, Sarah leaned into the mic.

"You all know the drill," she said. I watched in awe as every person in the room lowered their head, looking away from the stage and down at their feet. "You too, Chris, I can see you."

I looked down at the crusty bar floor as the opening bars of "Back to Before" played.

As she sang the opening line, I felt the warmth of her voice wash over the room. I recognized the song from her living room. I swear a collective sigh rose from the crowd. Glancing around, careful not to lift my head too high, I noticed that not a single head moved. Everyone continued to obey her request that they...not look at her?

It took every ounce of strength in my body not to look up, and I broke when she hit the final high note, my head snapping up of its own will. She had her eyes closed, both hands gripping the stand, leaned into it like she could loose any demons through the mesh wiring of the mic.

I was transfixed by her, unable to look away from the microscopic expressions of her face as she took a breath and stepped away. We had barely a moment of her eyes finding mine in the crowd before the entire room erupted into screaming applause. Her coworkers and the straggling strangers in the room all stood, whistling, clapping, stamping their feet like a rodeo crowd brought indoors. I launched to my feet, caught up by the fervor and the raw emotion I'd just witnessed from formerly wary Sarah.

If this was what she was capable of casually, I couldn't wait to see where she'd go as a pro.

SARAH

Chris's eyes caught mine at that last moment, that split second of song still lingering as the listener re-emerges to reality. But Chris never disappeared into the story. He stayed with me. Something about his gaze boosted me, made me plant my stance wider and grip the microphone a second time as applause died away.

"Can I do another one?" I asked. The approving roar that met me thudded into my chest, obliterating the crawling bugs and setting me free.

I whispered my choice to Marcus in the booth, ever-present Angie lurking over his shoulder.

The upbeat pop intro kicked off, and heads around the room bowed as if they expected Whitney Houston to forgive their sins. My heart clenched at their automatic movement, the deep respect they held for an embarrassing boundary I'd set years ago.

But tonight was different.

"You better get up and dance," I called out before launching into the opening of "I Wanna Dance with Somebody."

I threw myself into the song, letting my body move along to the beat and trilling riffs where I knew Whitney usually improvised. When we hit the key change at the bridge, I pulled the mic off the stand and began two-stepping across the stage while I continued. There wasn't a single still body in the room, every person singing along with me and dancing where they stood.

I spotted Chris and Angie dancing by the bar, his awkward shuffling no match for her hair-whipping twirls. In the last forty seconds of the song, I stepped off the stage, continuing to sing along into the mic and dancing in the crowd—just like I'd always seen the heroes do in movies.

I made my way across the room to Chris, my heart threatening to leap out of my chest as I got closer and closer to him. He stilled, watching me with a slightly slack-jawed, stunned expression, half a smile barely holding on. I hit the final notes, shimmying next to him and letting the microphone drop like a challenge when the song faded away.

Applause erupted a second time, mixed with screams and whistles. But they felt miles away as my world narrowed to just me and Chris, just the nearness of his lips to mine in that moment.

"Are we all gonna get to kiss Chris, too?" someone called out.

I realized with dawning horror that we'd leaned into each other and were now only a breath apart. Chris' eyes snapped open as he straightened. I thrust the microphone at him and stepped a whole-body length away.

"Your turn," I said as nonchalantly as if we were playing cards and not a more dangerous game.

"You're such a mood-ruiner, Janey," someone else called back across the room.

"That's not what you said last night," Janey called again.

"You better go pick a song before there's a kinda sexy riot," I said, turning on my heel and bolting for the door.

"Sarah, wait!" I heard Chris coming after me. Could I sprint home or would the superhero catch up to me? Only one way to find out.

The wet, cold air hit me like a wall, mist clinging to my hair, face, clothes. My feet slapped on the sidewalk, splashing filthy water up my pantleg and ankles, as my breath came harder and harder. I could hear matching footsteps behind me, heard Chris call my name again and again.

But I had the changing city on my side—a world he no longer recognized—and I ducked into an alley around the corner, watching him streak by from the shadows. I waited until I couldn't hear his thudding sprint anymore before stepping back out onto the street and heading for home.

The city was shimmering in the fog, all glittering, ghostly lights. My breath rose in steaming wisps, adding to the wet, thick cloud around me.

"What are you doing?" I asked myself as I turned onto my street, rubbing my hands up and down my arms to try and ward off the chill. "He probably dates models. And he's leaving after closing night anyway."

I let the building door slam behind me, unaware of the hour and the otherwise silent building.

"Trying to kiss someone you work with—an *actor* even," I kept muttering. My coffee Long Island was working on my system. I felt tipsy and energized, like my drunk heart was going to speed run the streets of San Francisco.

"That *does* seem pretty taboo," Chris' voice came from behind me.

"How long have you been there?"

"Depends," he said. "How long have you been talking to yourself?"

"Blocks," I said, frozen in place. "It's the coffee this late, makes me a little weird."

"Definitely just the coffee that does that," he said, huffing a half smile in my direction that made my stomach twist tighter than any megawatt magazine cover ever could. I wanted to throw myself at him. I wanted to turn and run inside and never leave my apartment again. I wanted to vanish on the spot. I wanted to kiss him so badly my chest physically pained with the need of it.

"Look, Sarah," he said, finally closing the distance between us. He ran his hands up my arms, tracing my shoulders so that I shivered. "I don't want to pressure you into anything, or rush anything, but..." His voice trailed off as he pushed his fingers up along my scalp, traversing my curls with an expertise I hadn't expected. We were barely a whisper apart now, all I had to do was flex my legs and we'd collide, lips tangling and—

"No more!"

We leapt apart as the door we were standing in front of swung open. Too late, I realized this was not my apartment. An elderly man stood in the doorway in his bathrobe, a half-empty PBR in one hand, a cane in the other.

"You two have been doing the will-they-won't-they dance in this hallway every morning," he said. "Now here you are! At night! I'm sick of it."

"Gerald!" A voice called from further back in the apartment. "Leave them alone! They're young and in love!"

"We're not—" I started.

Gerald held up the beer can for silence.

"I won't hear it anymore," he said. "Go inside and get it over with."

"Oh, real nice Gerald!" called the voice.

"Leave it, Betty," he hollered over his shoulder.

"We're sorry to bother you, sir, we'll be more courteous in the future."

"Not in the future," Gerald brandished his cane, gesturing down the hall. "*Now.*"

Chris nodded respectfully, then looped an arm around my waist and hauled me to our own doors as Gerald slammed his behind us.

"I guess this is goodnight," I said, standing in front of my own door.

"Sgt. Pepper will be disappointed," Chris said, sliding his keys from his pocket.

Down the hall, we heard a latch click open.

"Pick one already!" Gerald yelled, startling me into swinging my own door open and, without a second thought, pulling Chris in behind me.

As soon as my door swung shut, Chris' mouth was on mine, and it was as if the entire world was put on mute. The only sound was the pounding of my heart against my ribs and the hum in my veins.

And maybe a fantasy orchestra somewhere.

The kiss was gentle, but not careful, his lips questing hungrily over mine, hands cradling my face and neck. I felt held, cherished, but needed, as if I was the most beautiful glass of water he'd ever seen, but he'd been watching me from the desert. I ran my hands along Chris' chest, letting myself enjoy the shape of him, the way he was softer than I thought he'd be after all those oily shirtless photos on the internet. When my fingers grazed his nipples through his shirt, he let out a soft groan into my mouth then pulled me tighter to him, hands dropping from my face to grip my hips with a bruising heat.

Everything was his smell, his taste, his heat seeping into me and warming us both from the foggy night. I wanted more. I wanted to freeze time. I wanted the fastest way to remove clothing without ripping it. I wanted to hide from the possibility of this being the best thing that ever happened to me, and it would only be downhill from here.

Chris pulled away, leaning his forehead to mine, both of us breathing hard.

"Is this okay?" He asked, searching my face, eyes worried.

I nodded, but he paused, holding me in place.

"I'd like to hear your answer," he said, voice gentle.

"Yes," I croaked out. "Yes, it's okay. I think it's more than okay."

"Good," he grinned right at me and my stomach did cartwheels.

"Is it okay for you?" I asked, suddenly nervous that it might not be. The urge to hide grew stronger.

"More than okay," he said. "It's amazing." He kissed me again, and I wanted him to cherish every piece of me the way he doted on my mouth.

The kiss grew in intensity, need, heat. Chris slid warm hands along my waist, slipping beneath my shirt and skimming over the sensitive bare skin of my back. I arched into his touch, pressing myself against him anywhere I could, heat pooling between my legs and twisting into something heavier, needier, than a kiss could provide.

He answered my need, turning us and bracketing me between his arms, pressing me into my door. He was hard between my legs, breath ragged as he moved to my neck, and we ground into each other. But it was the gentle nip of his teeth on my shoulder that woke up the alarms.

"Wait," I gasped out, hating myself as relief shuddered through me at his immediate pause and step away. He didn't go far, eyes immediately on my face, hands on my shoulders.

"What's wrong?" He asked, voice ragged with need, eyes sparked with lust. I was going to *hate* myself in the morning.

"We should slow down," I said. "This could us both in a lot of trouble." Me more than him, most likely. And I definitely couldn't show up to work with hickeys after everyone saw us together at karaoke.

"Oh," he said, mouth lingering in an O shape for barely a moment. "Yes. Yes of course, you're right. We should. I'm sorry—"

"No, God don't be." *Please don't be sorry about me.* The bugs were back with a vengeance, rippling beneath my skin and burrowing into my joints. I fidgeted, I readjusted my clothes, I caved to their demands and wiggled out from Chris' arms even as my heart cried out at the distance.

"I don't want to do anything that would make you uncomfortable, Sarah," he said, shoving his hands into his jacket pockets and stepping away, putting even more distance between us.

"You didn't! I swear you didn't. I really, *really* liked...this." I gestured weakly between us. Somewhere in the back of my mind, a high-pitched keening was making it difficult to focus. I couldn't look at him, but I couldn't look away from him.

"But there's something wrong." He broke eye contact first, looking down at his feet, then to the door.

Don't let him go, a voice inside me shrieked, blocking out every other impulse I had.

"It's complicated," I said, hating how lame it sounded. "It's...I have a thing, and I haven't...no one else...just Angie I guess—"

Chris's warm hands covered mine, pulling it from the air where it'd been waving wildly and tracing soothing lines across it.

"I can do slow," he said, such kindness in his face I nearly burst into tears. In fact, my eyes burned, and heat tightened my chest. "I like slow, actually."

"Okay, good," I heaved a sigh, swiping obviously at my eyes with my free hand. "So, in that case, we should say goodnight."

"Goodnight, Sarah." He pressed a kiss to my knuckles, smiled at me, and slipped out the door, clicking it shut behind him.

Pressing a hand over my mouth, I let my knees give out and I sobbed silently on the floor. I was lightyears away from that scared 16-year-old girl and I was her all the time, simultaneously. Fear gripped me, threatening the same thing it always did—everyone would shun me, I'd be alone again, and there would be no starting over this time. There would be no running away to the big city, no apartment lottery that saved me from myself, no Angie in the wings to make me laugh when everything else threatened to swallow me.

The image of Chris asking me if this was okay, if I was okay, looped in my mind. I took deeper breaths, wiped my face on my sleeves, settled with my back against the door for a second time.

"I *am* okay." My voice fell into my lap, the silent apartment refusing the statement. And I was.

Chris and I were *both* adults. And no one at CAT could claim he was playing favorites—he had no control over anything at the theatre. Here, he was just another actor, not Captain Arrow Star, Hollywood hero.

Things could be different than what my fear and anxiety predicted. I'd make sure of it.

"What if someone sees?"

I was holding hands with Chris Oldfelds. I was holding hands with Chris Oldfelds on the *street* in *public*.

Never mind that we were fulfilling one of my biggest dating fantasies of strolling through San Francisco in the morning, holding hands and sipping coffee—I was doing it with the most handsome man who had ever been into me *in my life.*

I hated to admit it, but I was a little starstruck.

"Let them," he said, pulling me under his arm and continuing to stroll down the hill with his arm on my shoulders—as if we did this all the time.

We'd met in the hall that morning, shy, unsure, bashful. Chris pointed out that handholding was pretty chaste—exactly what a slow-moving romance needed—and I'd happily conceded.

Men who were out to ruin your reputation didn't offer to hold hands.

"Aren't the tabloids going to chase you?" My head was on a swivel, sure that everyone would know I'd broken coworker and normal not-Hollywood citizen lines alike.

"I'm not that important right now," he said. "The franchise is over, and the fifth movie flopped."

"You never told me why you took such a low-paying gig," I said as we turned the corner. The sun ducked behind buildings and the air chilled. I leaned into Chris a little closer, letting my steps zig zag to avoid getting tangled.

"I wanted to, and I could," he said. "So, I did."

"That's a cop-out," I said, smacking his chest playfully.

"I have to maintain an air of mystery, or you'll find out I'm actually boring," he teased.

"Please tell me," I said. "I'll keep it a secret, I swear." I was giddy, high on life, absolutely elated. So, I didn't understand why suddenly Chris stepped away, stopping both of us on the street. He looked away from me, a distant pain in his eyes.

"I haven't been back since my mom died," he said. "The last time I was on a stage she was healthy, cheering me on from the front row.

She loved when I did live shows. When Alan called with the part, I felt like this was her asking for one last hometown performance."

My heart broke on the sidewalk as I reached over to squeeze his hand.

"I'm so sorry, Chris," I said.

He squeezed back, avoiding my eyes.

"I couldn't think why else Alan would call me out of the blue and offer me the part without an audition," he said. "He was always so committed to local actors getting paid work—I'm not exactly a local anymore."

His bright blue eyes returned to mine, and staying there, softening around the edges.

"Man, I'm glad I did."

"You say that to all the PAs," I joked.

His face grew serious.

"I don't, Sarah," he said. "There is only you and there has only been you since I got here. I haven't spent any time with anyone else, much less in the crew."

"I didn't—"

"It's really important that's made clear," he said. I wasn't sure I liked how stern he sounded.

"I was joking, first of all," I said dropping his hand. "But you're clearly not."

"It's just..." He shuffled on the sidewalk, and I realized I wasn't the only one worried about rumors and opinions. I waited, trying to give him the same grace he'd given me last night.

"Leon said some things when I went out with the other actors, and then Rebecca joined in and—"

"Leon sleeps with a new costumer every time we get one," I cut him off. "Whatever he said to you, ignore it."

Chris' shoulders dropped, a sigh huffing free. "I don't want to be like that," he said. "And I don't want anyone to think you're mixed up with just another egotistical actor."

"You're *not* like that," I said. "And if anyone has a problem with your ego, send them to me."

"Cause you're so scary," he laughed.

"Seriously, Chris," I said. "Whatever it is we're doing, it'll only work as long as we don't let other people's opinions interfere." I needed to hear that as much as he did. I just couldn't believe it was coming out of *my* mouth.

He rolled his shoulders back and stuck his hand out to me in a businessman stance.

"Deal," he said.

I took his hand and shook it.

"Deal."

If only it was that easy.

Chris

"**I** heard a juicy little tidbit."

I braced myself as Leon swaggered into the theatre, untying his endlessly long scarf and flipping his hair from his face. I've never been a violent person—usually got beat up on the playground instead of fighting back—but there was something in Leon's permanent sneer and quirked eyebrow that made me want to punch him.

"Not today, Leon," Nicole said without looking up from her script.

"We've got a long day ahead of us, dear, let's save gossip for drinks later." Rebecca was perched on a set piece, primly flipping script pages as if she were looking for a line she missed.

I rolled my eyes and sipped the coffee Sarah had made me that morning. In the silence that followed, Leon waited, and I made the mistake of yawning. I'd been up all night thinking about Sarah—kissing her, how she'd asked to slow down, kissing her more, doing more than kissing her.

But my yawn was damning to Leon.

"If *some* people stopped making out with the crew, then they might have more energy." Leon set his bags down on the stage with a flourish. He was looking straight at me, but I refused to give him the satisfaction.

I arched my eyebrows at him, holding his gaze. I put on a bored act, hoping it smothered the immediate panic that gripped my stomach.

"Is this your way of telling us you took another costumer home?" I asked.

A chorus of gasps rang out from the rest of the cast. Leon's face purpled, and I realized too late I'd poked the bear.

"Pot kettle black," he hissed. "Kissing Sarah in a karaoke bar last night."

"Actually, it was in her apartment," I corrected. "If you're going to gossip about me, get your facts straight."

"She's a sweet girl," Nicole said, giving me an approving thumbs up.

"Really, Christopher," Rebecca clucked her teeth and shook her head.

"It's just Chris, and yes, really."

"Alright, everyone, gather round please, I have a few notes," Alan interrupted the staring contest I was having with Leon, forcing both of us to get a grip as rehearsal kicked off.

I didn't think announcing our new romance to the entire cast was what Sarah meant by slowing down, but I knew the only way to stop any bullying in its tracks was to own the thing they were trying to nitpick. Unfortunately, it seemed all I'd done was motivate Leon to find something else to needle. His enraged glare never left my face as Alan gave notes.

As we broke from the circle to stretch, warm up, and begin another scene, Leon brushed by me, roughly jostling my shoulder.

"Just wait 'till you leave," he hissed. "Things will go back to the way they're supposed to be—where true talent is rewarded. My friends at the top have already made sure of that."

"Is that a threat, Leon?" I asked, letting my voice carry across the stage. Leon froze, taking in all the eyes trained directly on him.

"Gentlemen," Alan said, voice a low warning.

"No, you know what Alan, this is bullshit." Leon whirled on the director, body and voice trembling with rage. "You give all this lip service to hiring local talent, focusing on keeping art in the city, 'we're only as good as what we reinvest in.'" I hated him for mocking Alan's mission. My fingers flexed against my palm, as if my hand could fly off my body and complete its own violent objective.

"We do." Alan crossed his arms, arched his eyebrows, waited.

"Sure we do." Leon threw an arm in my direction. "Cause bringing in millionaires is reinvesting in our community."

"Chris grew up—"

"I don't give a flying fuck where he grew up, he's not local anymore. He's LA through and through—look at him."

I couldn't help glancing at my feet, my face burning.

"But I see what you're doing." He crept across the stage, getting exactly what he wanted now—every pair of eyes in the building was trained on him now, giving him focus, the tension in the air thickening as I felt the press of more and more bodies peering from the wings. "You don't want anyone else to know, so you wrap it up in the excuse of a good ol' pal coming home again. But I know." He thumped a fist against his chest. "I know that we're failing. That bringing in outside talent is your attempt to attract an audience that wants nothing to do with us anymore."

"Everyone on this stage—"

"'Earned their spot.' Save it, Alan. We all know your stupid fucking sayings at this point. But only I know they're bullshit."

Leon took in the attention he had now, the way everyone was holding their breath to see what he'd say next. I had the sudden nasty thought that he'd never give a performance this good again, and he knew it.

"What about the next production? Will everyone have earned their spot on stage?"

Alan opened his mouth, but Leon plowed over him.

"I know one little songbird who will have earned it through *unsavory* means."

"Stop right there, Leon, I have *never—*"

The actor flung yet another angry hand in my direction. This time it stayed, fingers twisted into an accusatory point, trembling in the stage lights.

"King Chris screws a stagehand, and she gets an audition out of nowhere? And I'm just supposed to believe those two things aren't related?" It was as if he flung the words directly at my chest, but this time, they hit their mark.

Alan's eyebrows shot so high on his head they were in danger of flying off.

"I was unaware of anyone's involvement romantically with their coworkers," Alan said slowly. "And any auditions given are my call and mine alone. You know that better than anyone, Leon."

"What is *that* supposed to mean?" His jaw dropped. A vein pulsed in his forehead. Somewhere, in the far depth of the wings, I heard a soft giggle.

"I think you know," Alan replied, calmly flipping pages in his folio. "Let's return to our work. You and I can speak privately after.

"I can't believe—you're just going to let him do whatever he wants," Leon seethed. "Aren't you?"

Silence stretched across the stage like suffocating layers of plastic wrap.

Was Alan bending to me?

"There are no laws preventing like-minded members of this production from mingling with each other in whatever capacity," Alan said, voice strained. He'd pushed his glasses to the top of his head—an alarming signal I'd only seen once before when he chewed out an actor for pointing a prop gun *at* someone instead of *next* to them. "As much as *some people* think they're above the work our talented crew does to keep the show running smoothly. You should be so lucky as to receive the affections of a dedicated, capable PA." He leveled a searing gaze at the rest of the cast. "Any of you."

"Hell yeah," Nicole called, pumping a fist in the air.

"Aren't you married?" Rebecca asked primly.

"Not that married," Nicole snapped, eyeing Rebecca suggestively until the older woman dropped her gaze.

"It's a power imbalance," Leon whined. "He's taking—"

"Like you give a shit, Leon," a voice called from the wings. An athletic blonde woman with pronounced freckles and a stern hand on her hip stepped into the dim lighting.

"It's not like that, Marisol, I—"

"Save it."

"Thank you, Marisol. Thank you, everyone." Alan said pointedly, gesturing back to the script. "If we could refocus our attention. I love *Kissing Strangers to Get Married* as much as any of you, but I don't plan on hosting a special in our theatre. We are here to *work*."

The blonde woman—Marisol, apparently—nodded curtly to Alan and shot a death glare at Leon, her fuming gaze not leaving his even as she turned and disappeared back into the wings.

The rest of us took our places, I was only vaguely aware of Nicole and Rebecca beginning the scene. The words waved on the page and the edges of my vision burned.

"Whatever," I heard Leon grumble. In a whirlwind of floppy hair and black clothing, he snatched up his things and tore out of the theatre. We all finally paused when the house doors slammed.

"Oh dear," Alan said, adjusting his glasses. "Someone call Tyler. We'll need him to fill in."

And with that, rehearsal started.

I couldn't focus. I missed several cues, messed up the lines I'd memorized, and somehow bungled the ones I read on book.

Sarah was auditioning. Sarah and I were seeing each other. I was maybe here as a publicity stunt. I couldn't wait for Alan to see what she could do, but more than that, selfishly, I couldn't wait to hear her voice again. I was relieved to still be on the stage after Leon's tantrum. I doubted my place there for the first time in my life.

Guilt and confusion warred in my chest. Just because Leon was the loudest dissenter in the room didn't make him the only one.

I didn't want anything to jeopardize Sarah's audition—not when she had so much promise, when she'd been so brave to ask for it. I could already hear her justifying why she should back out.

And if my membership in the cast was truly a tactic and not an invitation to make great art with my fellow actors, then maybe bowing out was the only way to ensure Sarah's chance and my pride didn't get hurt in the same swing.

"Okay," Alan sighed after a frustrating few hours. "Everyone take a lunch. Chris, come back ready to focus."

I nodded, deciding to take lunch alone. I could use a long walk to blow off some steam and try to get my focus back.

When I opened the side door to the theatre, all my plans were dashed. Paparazzi flashed cameras and hollered questions. I was momentarily blinded, frozen in place, overwhelmed by the overlapping, demanding voices.

"Who is Sarah Aguilar?"

"Tell us about your new girlfriend!"

"Is it serious?"

"Is she going to follow your career or are you staying here?"

"Are you staying in San Francisco, Chris?"

"How serious is the relationship?"

The questions flurried around me, creating a wall of noise and lights that I couldn't break past.

Then, just as suddenly as it started, it ended. I blinked, letting my eyes adjust to the dark of the theatre. Someone had closed the door. The smattering of microphone pieces on the floor told me exactly who intervened on my behalf.

Sarah put a comforting hand on my shoulder, a half-mocking smile on her face. Relief flooded me at the same time guilt crashed in, hauling my heart to my stomach.

"You sure it didn't matter that we held hands this morning?"

"That wouldn't have caused this," I said shaking my head, trying to make sense of the reporters' shouts. "Someone leaked it."

"Don't stress about it too much, the theatre has security for this exact reason," she said, running her hand up and down my arm. I leaned into the touch, pulling her into a tight hug.

"I'm supposed to be coming home, I didn't want a security detail," I sighed into her curls. "I'll have my guys fly up from LA tonight."

Sarah tilted her head up from where I'd been accidentally squishing her into my chest.

"I'm sorry you have to deal with this," she said.

"Me too," I said. "And you, too. You'll have to stick close to me now that people know your name. I don't want anything to happen to you because we got involved."

"I don't think anything will," she said. "Besides, I've got Captain Arrow Star to protect me." She gave me a wink. I leaned down and kissed the top of her head.

"People are staring," she said, taking a quick step back from and breaking contact.

I was going to tease her but noticed the heat in her face and the way she shifted from foot to foot. As much as I didn't want to, I let her go.

I turned around to the gathered cast and crew who apparently watched us fight off paparazzi and snuggle.

"Guess I have to get delivery," I said and shrugged dramatically. Alan was on his phone behind everyone else, his frantic murmuring punctuating the silence. No one else said anything. I scanned the worried faces gathered near me and Sarah. Finally, I let out a deep breath.

"Alright, who *else* wants delivery?"

The delivery guy needed a police escort to get through the front doors, but after two hours of waiting, we had the best Nepalese food in the country.

Sarah and Angie hauled tables out from the back and the prop master found plates and silverware for everyone.

I was starving, having spent what was supposed to be my lunch break fielding calls from my agent, manager, and security detail. Sarah's mom called her, and she'd spent the better part of an hour murmuring soothing-sounding Spanish into the phone.

Apparently, someone called in a tip to every tabloid at the supermarket that not only did I have a new girlfriend, but I'd slept with half the crew at the theatre. It didn't stop there. I was also a sex addict, preying on cast and crew alike on the set of every movie I'd ever done.

They were claiming that my sexual appetite was the sole reason for the termination of the Captain Arrow Star movie franchise.

More reporters than I'd ever seen in my life showed up outside the theatre, surrounding all the exits—including the narrow alley Sarah guided me through last time. James and Greg, my security guys, were on the next flight from LA and would be at the theatre before the end of the day.

"Alright everyone," Alan clapped his hands together as cast and crew gathered around the tables bowing under the weight of momos, curries, and biryani. "Let's feast. And then it's back to work, hive-mind photographer beasts bearing down upon us or not."

A ripple of laughter rang through the theatre, and I could feel the tension in the air begin to melt away thanks to good food.

The momos were perfect, steamed to doughy perfection and filled with flavorful, spiced meat and vegetables. The potato curry melted in my mouth and left a pleasant burn as it went down.

"I'm never going back to Hollywood," I announced, patting my full stomach. "I'll miss food too much."

"And Sarah," Angie chimed in, grunting when Sarah smacked her immediately after.

"Ignore her," she said to me, and then repeated it again to the watchful eyes around the room. Every set of eyes but mine. My gut twisted around the Nepalese feast I'd just devoured, threatening to send it back up. I didn't want us to be ruined before we had a chance to start.

Before I could pull Sarah aside, the tables were cleared away, the food polished off, and Alan was clapping his hands again to kick off the rest of rehearsal.

I threw myself into the show, shifting into my character and letting the real world fall away. It was a rare day that I remembered why I got into acting in the first place, and it felt good to have that feeling back. I was no long Chris Oldfelds, movie actor and stressed-out potential boyfriend. I was Harry Stratford, conflicted husband and Communist sympathizer.

All too soon, however, the house doors opened, and I looked up to see two familiar muscled friends dressed all in black following the House manager down the aisle.

I threw them a wave as Alan continued giving notes to the gathered cast.

"Excellent work today, Chris," he said, coming to me last. "Great return to focus in the second half, and I appreciate the choices you're making with Harry. Try not to reach emotional climax so fast in your monologue in scene four, otherwise you won't have anywhere to go for the minutes that follow afterward."

I nodded, scribbling in my notes. Alan sighed, pushing his glasses to the top of his head.

"Alright everyone, Dorian is going to work on releasing us in small groups. Do not engage with anyone outside. Chris has lent us his extended security detail for escorts home if anyone is afraid of being followed."

Whispers and shuffling feet sounded across the theatre as we broke to go home. Nicole found me, squeezing my hand.

"Be careful," she said. "We like having you here, we'd hate to lose you already."

"I'm not going anywhere," I said. That was a promise.

SARAH

"Well, it was nice working with you." Rebecca came up to me as the last of the crew cleared out, following Dorian like a gaggle of ducklings through the house doors.

"Excuse me?" I looked if anyone else was listening and, for the first time all day, they weren't.

"Well, you've bagged a movie star," she purred. "Surely you're not going to keep working at our little non-profit theatre anymore."

"I love it here," I said, taking a step back from her. "And I haven't 'bagged' anyone."

"We all see the way you two look at each other," she said, rolling her eyes. "It's disgusting. I won't be surprised if you're married before the year is up so you can really lock it in. Whatever spell you've got him under, good for you."

Rage boiled hot in my gut, threatening to bubble up and out of my mouth with words I knew I'd regret. But before it could spew out, Alan appeared over Rebecca's shoulder.

"Sarah," he said, waving at me and stepping around Rebecca. "I've been looking for you. I spoke with Paul and he'll most likely be swapping the order of our season. Very last minute, I'm sorry, but it means potentially big things for you. I'd like to move your audition up if we could."

I nodded dumbly, barely registering the mention of the company's artistic director.

"Would the fourth be okay?"

Again, I nodded. That was in two weeks. I'd only have two weeks to prepare.

"Thanks for being flexible," Alan said. "And be careful this week, okay?"

He stepped away, calling someone else's name and hurrying toward them.

"Oh," Rebecca said, giving me a knowing look. "So that's what it's about then."

"I don't —"

"You don't have to play dumb with me," she said, winking. My stomach churned. "I admire a gal with ambition. Good luck."

She threw the theatre curse over her shoulder as she walked away, meeting Dorian halfway up the aisle.

We *never* said "good luck" in the theatre. We always wished each other calamity—break a leg, for example—so we didn't have disastrously unlucky performances. It was as if we could trick Lady Luck herself by refusing to invoke her name.

I was broken from my shocked state by Chris' hand on my shoulder.

"You ready?" he asked, concern creasing his handsome face.

"I think Rebecca hates me," I said without thinking.

"She hates herself more," he said, a smile softening his face.

Chris' security guys met us among the seats, introducing themselves as James and Greg. James was the tallest man I'd ever seen, built like a refrigerator box with dark tattoos twisting up each arm and disappearing into his black t-shirt. Greg was only about six inches shorter than him with an impressive V-shaped torso I thought only existed on action figures. A single gold hoop dangled from one ear. They both shook my hand and nodded wordlessly in greeting.

"Remember," Chris said, looping a protective arm around my shoulders. "They *want* you to say something to them. Anything. And they'll say anything to get a response from you because it gives them more selling power with the photos. Don't give them what they want."

I nodded. This was quickly becoming too much—the stares and whispers all day, the paparazzi, my audition moved up. I wanted to lay down on the House carpet and not move until it was all over.

"I'm right here with you, okay?" He looked down at me and it took everything in me not to burst into tears. "All we have to do is get across the sidewalk and into the car."

"That feels like walking across the ocean," I said, embarrassed at the trembling in my voice.

"Moses did it," he said and grinned at me. "How hard could it be?"

"Don't let go," I said. His arm felt like shelter against a natural disaster.

Chris squeezed my shoulders and then nodded to James and Greg. They stood on either side of us as we made our way through the theatre. Dorian was in the lobby, waiting for us with the complimentary umbrellas we used to guide guests into taxis on rainy days.

"Here," he said, opening one and handing it to me. "The gift shop is out of hats at the moment, this was all I could find."

The front doors, usually floor to ceiling glass that let in the slanted sunshine had been covered in butcher paper. It made the lobby look like it was haunted by some unnamed phantom.

My heart slammed into my throat and my breath came in shallow gasps. I clung onto Chris' hand as James and Greg opened the doors, leveling the umbrella directly in front of us, obscuring us from the hungry cameras.

The noise hit me like a wall. I couldn't focus on anything but the press of bodies all around—Chris on one side, Greg on the other, and hundreds of strangers lined up too close, waiting to crush in for the perfect, million-dollar photograph.

Our steps slowed, and I felt Greg shift next to me, pressing his back to the screaming photographers. He put a soft hand on my upper back, guiding me forward with a ghost of a touch. Chris' hand never left mine, no matter how sweaty it got.

"Who is your new girlfriend?"

"Is she better than the others?"

"Tell us how you met!"

"She's hot, good job!"

"Give us a smile, sweetie!"

"How's it feel to bag a movie star?"

"Whatever you did, keep doing it, baby!"

"You're going places now!"

The last one got to me. I felt the dig burrow beneath my skin like that creature from The Matrix, each articulated leg stabbing into me.

My breath came fast and shallow. My head swam. I felt the tell-tale pull on my stomach that told me I was about to have a flashback—I was about to feel split between worlds, one half in the present day, one half on the worst day of my life.

"You're really gonna be famous now, huh?" she sneered as she slammed her locker door closed, blonde braid swinging with not a hair out of place. "Sleeping your way to the top like all the other Hollywood sluts. You'll fit right in."

Whispers fled down the hall, catching fire from person to person, eyes glued to me and Olivia.

"Liv, I—"

"Word to the wise, Sarah," she readjusted her grip on her textbook and binder, pressing them close to her chest. "I don't think every Broadway star fucked their choir teacher. You might want to reconsider your strategy."

She was gone before I could defend myself, leaving me dumbstruck and mortified in a completely silent school hallway. Even a few teachers stuck their heads out of their classrooms to see what kind of chaos was happening.

"Alright, everyone to your classes, no lingering." The voice froze me to the spot.

A car door shut, and the sudden muffled silence brought me back to reality. I gasped for breath, leaning over my knees until the stars faded from my vision.

Chris ran a hand over my back in soothing circles as we pulled away from the curb.

I needed to be home. I needed my dark, quiet apartment with the leaky faucet and the weird stain on the ceiling. I'd even eat more rice and beans if it meant no one would yell at me for the next few hours. Hope filtered through my thoughts, rising to the top like pasta in boiling water, as we pulled away from the theatre. It was a short commute already, made even shorter by car.

Just as quickly as it arrived, hope disappeared.

Photographers and reporters were three deep on the sidewalk, blocking anyone from walking by and heckling any neighbor that dared to come and go. Guilt swept over me like a crashing wave, threatening to pull me under. This was *home*—for me and for all my neighbors. And now I'd brought this mess to our literal front door.

A screaming voice pulled our attention to the third-floor window where Gerald was halfway out, shaking his fist in the air.

"Fuck off, ya vultures!"

"To the Ritz, please," Chris said, as casually as if he'd just asked the driver to drop us at BART.

My jaw dropped as I tore my gaze away from Gerald, who was now flinging empty beer cans into the crowd.

"To where now?"

Chris looked slightly embarrassed, and my heart stuttered at the sweet blush that bloomed across his cheeks—it was that or anxiety. Who knew at this point.

"They're prepared for stuff like this," he said, waving a hand through the air. "You know I'd rather stay at the apartment."

"I don't know that actually," I said. It suddenly felt like I didn't know Chris at all, and I realized, because he'd been staying across the hall from me in my beloved but rundown apartment building, I'd failed to connect the dots between "movie star" and "has a lot of money."

"It's just until this mess dies down," he said.

"Or you'll get comfortable and never go back to the apartment."

"I have to go back to the apartment," he said, voice quiet.

"Why'd you request it in the first place?" I asked, desperate for a distraction from the chaos outside, from the hammering in my chest, from the guilt threatening to pull me through the floor of the car.

"Promise you won't think it's weird?"

The car climbed a hill, and the late sunshine slanted across his face. There, still, was the honest look, the completely open face.

"I grew up in that apartment," he said. "I wanted to come back one last time."

"And the woman who was living there?" I'd been too wrapped up in Chris' appearance on my doorstep that night to even revisit the fact that Amanda, the 21-year-old Black lounge singer, aerialist, and part-time dog walker who'd lived across from me for three years, was nowhere to be found.

"Staying with family in Oakland," he said. "I'm subletting from her while I'm here."

"Sir, we're here," the driver said as we pulled into the sloped driveway of the Ritz Carlton.

I'd only ever seen the building from a distance, perched on one of San Francisco's steeper hills just a few blocks from the Financial District. It was all white, glowing in the sun. Neat rows of windows and Greek pillars caught my eye as a white-gloved door man opened the door for me and helped me from the car.

I followed Chris into the lush lobby where we were immediately joined at a quick pace by the hotel manager. He was a short man in an expensive suit who talked and walked with his hands clutched behind his back. He spoke mostly with Chris, giving me a polite nod. I'd never felt so out of place in my life in my paint-splattered Dickies and volunteering t-shirt.

I would've dressed differently if I'd known my day would end at the Ritz.

Strings sang out from the restaurant as we passed, where people enjoyed cocktails and appetizers in a gorgeously arranged parlor. A quartet played in the corner, wearing all black—the standard industry uniform. No one else noticed that the musicians matched the servers matched the cooks matched the hospitality staff smiling from behind the desk. I thought about my stage blacks—the all-black outfit crew wore to avoid drawing attention to themselves during performances. Maybe I should've joined the serving staff instead of following Chris into the brass elevator.

"Jesus," I whispered as the doors closed and we were finally alone.

"Yeah," was all Chris said.

The elevator opened on a silent carpeted hall. Doors lined each wall, but unlike our—*my*—apartment building, there was no clamoring TV or conversation leaking out through the cracks. Because there were no cracks. There was no tenant art hung crooked against peeling walls, no familiar work boots left in the hall, no voices bumping and crashing against each other, providing the minimal comfort that at least we weren't alone.

We reached a door on the far end of the hall and Chris tapped a keycard against it, hinges silent as it whooshed open to reveal a massive, lush room.

There was a TV and sofa in a designated area to one side and a massive king bed with crisp, fluffy white linens on the other. I could barely hear my own steps in the plush carpeting as I walked to the window and looked out over the city.

Suddenly, it was all too much. I burst into tears.

"It's just for one night," Chris said, voice tense. "I'm so sorry I didn't want you to have to deal with this. I'll sleep on the couch. You can have the bed—"

"Alan moved my audition up," I croaked out around sobs. Chris found a box of tissues and brought them to me, holding the box as I pulled one out and shoved my face in it.

"Why?"

"He said they were re-scheduling the show order at the last minute," I sobbed. I was crying so hard now I started hiccupping. "And it was a big opportunity for me and could we do it in two weeks."

"You'll be amazing whenever your audition is," Chris said, awkwardly squeezing my shoulder.

"And now I'm ugly crying in front of you," I said, trying to hide in the crumbled tissue. Chris gently pried it from my hand and handed me a fresh one.

"You're never ugly," he said.

"You don't know that!" I threw my hands in the air and started to walk around the room, letting my nervous energy work off through the carpet. "Just like I don't know if you actually live like this all the time."

"Sarah—"

"And I don't know if I'm just another PA that you've seduced," I threw my hands in the air, all the worries I'd been holding onto flying out of my mouth. "I don't know if I'll ever see you again after the show closes. And I don't know if I can handle this."

"What do you mean?"

"The photographers, and the staring, and the Jameses and Gregs," I said, storming back to him and taking a new tissue. He was still standing in place, holding the tissue box and looking at me. He was looking at me with those perfect blue eyes, his mouth a tight line. I watched a muscle in his jaw tick.

"I'm not made for all this," I continued. "I'm backstage for a *reason*."

He was silent, lips pursed tight as I slowly calmed down until I was reduced to sniffles and hiccups. I opened my mouth to apologize for all the emotional dumping, but Chris cut me off.

"You're made for so much more than hiding in the wings, Sarah." His voice was soft but strained, and there was a new emotion on his face I couldn't name. "As much as you say you're not made for all this," he gestured between us with the tissue box. "I think you're wrong."

I sniffled.

"I wasn't made for this either but..." He stopped suddenly and a strange look crossed his face.

"You don't have to lie to me," I said, letting my shoulders drop. Defeat settled in swiftly, like so many birds to a tree in a storm.

"I've seen all different types of people find their opportunity," he said finally. "This is just a bump in the road." He pulled me in for a tight hug, warm and comforting, smelling a little muskier than his normal bright, clean scent.

I let myself sink into him.

"It'll be alright," he said. "You'll see."

Chris

We were made for each other.

The words hadn't stopped bouncing around my head since I forced myself not to say them.

"I wasn't made for this either, but we were made for each other."

They echoed while Sarah and I ordered room service, sharing burgers and fries on the couch while we flipped through a hundred different channels. They ricocheted when, after the fourth re-run episode, Sarah leaned her head on my shoulder and began snoring lightly. They wouldn't stop repeating on a loop as I nudged Sarah awake and guided her to the bed, tucking her in carefully before coming back to the couch.

And now, here I was, lying awake staring at the dark ceiling, listening to Sarah's steady breathing, and wishing I knew how to reconcile the truth of those words with the reality we were living.

We were made for each other.

But we were barely more than strangers.

I didn't know it 'till I said it, but I wouldn't have said it if I didn't mean it. I was a lot of things as an actor, but a liar wasn't one of them. Good acting, I'd been taught, was finding the truth of a moment and using that for fuel.

And this was truth—blinding, sharp, brilliant, uncomfortable, unbelievable truth.

I rolled onto my side and stared at the black screen of the TV. Alan had already told us the show order was being reworked. But what did that mean for our lunch conversation the first day where he'd said he'd find another part for me if I wanted to stay? And how did that relate to my possible tenure as a publicity stunt? I still hadn't been able to catch him one-on-one to ask. He'd dodged my calls and ignored my texts since leaving the theatre.

More importantly, what did this mean for Sarah? I knew she was nervous about the audition. I knew it'd taken every ounce of her courage to agree to it, knew something chased her I couldn't see or know until she let me. She'd said she stayed in the wings on purpose—hidden, safe—but I hoped, someday soon, she'd step out of them and onto the stage where she deserved to be.

Only time could tell, and unfortunately, it was starting to feel like time was the one thing we didn't have.

"I don't know if I'll ever see you again after the show closes." She'd said it with tears streaming down her face, frustration pulling her mouth into a tight line. I'd been so intent on chasing my feelings for Sarah I hadn't considered how this would all play out. I didn't know where I'd be or where I'd go when the show closed. Sure, I could take a break, but my career was at the perfect space where I could do more exploring of my art instead of taking the best paid gig. I worried I'd lose that balance if I stepped away from LA for too long.

But San Francisco wasn't so far. Maybe, if things worked out—

I stopped myself. I could *not* move cities for a woman I'd kissed once and known barely a week.

But I *would*. Already, I knew that if she woke up right now and asked me to move to San Francisco to continue our budding relationship, I'd do it in a heartbeat. My pulse kicked up, and I rubbed my sweating palms on the thin throw blanket. This was not going to help me fall asleep.

I closed my eyes, rolled back over, and started to clear my mind with an exercise I'd learned on set. I started counting, thinking only of the numbers, starting over every time another thought intervened and threatened to distract me.

Slowly, I began to relax, feeling sleepier and sleepier.

I finally dozed off, but it only felt like moments before Sarah's voice woke me, shouting something incoherent. It took me several dazed moments, already halfway to her bedside, before I realized she was yelling in her sleep.

I shook her lightly, whispering her name.

Her eyes snapped open, and she looked at me over her shoulder as if she'd never seen me before. She exhaled in a whoosh before rubbing her face.

"You were having a nightmare," I explained. She nodded.

"Sorry," she whispered.

"Don't apologize," I said. "It's okay." I squeezed her shoulder and went to walk away, back to the couch, but Sarah reached over and grabbed my hand.

"Stay," she said. "Please."

"You sure?" I asked. She tugged on my hand with surprising strength, nearly knocking me off balance. I grinned despite myself, following her insistence. I pulled the covers back, curling around her warmth and settling onto the pillow next to her. We weren't exactly in the middle of the bed, but I didn't mind.

As her breathing evened out, my eyes grew heavy, and my heart settled into rhythm with hers. I fell asleep there, with Sarah in my arms, in a massive plush bed, thinking about nothing else but the rise and fall of her breaths.

The next morning, I woke before Sarah, carefully sliding my arm out from under her head. Light peeked through the thick curtains, spreading tendrils across the carpet.

I clicked on the bathroom light, wincing at its brightness, and ran the shower, wishing I'd asked James to drop off a few things at the hotel after I'd sent him to check on Sgt. Pepper. Putting on dirty clothes after getting clean always bothered me.

Sarah still wasn't up, and I remembered how frazzled she always looked when we met for coffee in the mornings. She must've been doing me a favor, showing me around that early.

I felt a tingle in my chest at this intimate piece of knowledge. I liked knowing things about her, even small bites of her habits or mannerisms.

Stepping into the hall, I broke my morning rules and looked at my phone while waiting for the elevator. Several news alerts with my name in them were at the top of my inbox. The first and second headlines were what I expected—was I a creep? Had I been taking advantage of crew this whole time? They speculated but did little to confirm. That was where Leon messed up. There was no one else to lie with him.

But the third headline made me hold my breath.

"Smolders Likes Em Spicy: Details on the Heartthrob's New Feisty Latina Lover." The elevator dinged. I clicked the link. I let loose a relieved sigh.

Aside from a few photos of me and Sarah walking around San Francisco, the article had very little text—not even so much as her first name.

We were okay for now.

Stepping into the elevator, I pocketed my phone, trying to find the quiet joy I'd been basking in. But I couldn't help feeling guilty all over again for the chaos I'd brought to Sarah's door—to the theatre's door, literally. I made a mental note to call my PR team after breakfast. Maybe there was some extension of coverage or support they could offer.

The breakfast buffet in the member's lounge was bustling with activity, waiters pinging around the room like pinballs on a course for destruction. Businessmen talked loudly into their earpieces or phones, spooning eggs and bacon onto tiny ceramic plates.

Coffee came from one of those all-in-one espresso machines, and I realized suddenly I didn't know how Sarah took her coffee after a week of mornings together. Black to start. We could go from there.

I hummed to myself as I tucked sugar packets into my pocket, holding two cups of coffee in one hand, a pitcher of creamer in the other.

"Still got it," I said to myself as I swerved away from a waiter with my delivery. Every actor has worked food service at one point or another, and I was no exception. I'd waited tables in a breakfast place in LA when I was first getting started, and I was prouder than expected to see my carrying skills stuck around. That job, and so many others, felt like a lifetime ago compared to where I was and what I was doing now.

But it still felt important—like it'd been a rite of passage that put me in good company.

Upstairs, Sarah had rolled over to the middle of the bed. I set the coffees down and sat at the edge, nudging her gently.

She sat up with a roaring snort and rubbed her face as she looked around. Her curls were wild around her face, framing her like a cushy halo, and there was a bit of sleep crusting her left eye. My heart clenched at how much I wanted to reach over and smooth her hair, clear the gunk from her face, kiss each cheek before she was fully awake.

"I brought coffee," I said.

She smiled at me, soft, bright, warm. "You're my favorite person today," she said.

"Just today?" I teased, offering her a cup. I waited, watching her face as she looked around before I pulled the sugar from my pockets and handed her the creamer.

"Yessss," she hissed happily. "Now you'll be my favorite person tomorrow too."

"How do I get to be your favorite person for more than a day at a time," I asked, kicking my shoes off and settling on the bed next to her with my own black coffee.

"Be made of black licorice."

I laughed so hard my coffee nearly shot from my nose.

"Black licorice?" I asked. "That's so gross."

"It's not. It's the best candy in the world and everyone who disagrees doesn't know what they're missing," she huffed, sipping her coffee.

"Wow," I said, feeling my face split into a grin. "You are one of a kind, Sarah Aguilar."

She shrugged, smiling back. "Says the man with a history-making movie deal."

I rolled my eyes. "Everyone has one of those," I teased. "Not everyone likes black licorice. On purpose. Are you sure you weren't tortured into submission by the black licorice lobby?"

She laughed. I could've eaten the sound from the air.

My phone rang, interrupting our domestic moment.

"Hi Alan," I answered, looking at Sarah with my eyebrows arched.

"Chris," Alan's voice was tense through the phone. "We're cancelling rehearsals for the day. The theatre is beset."

I sighed.

"It's not your fault," he said. "I'm going to have serious words with Leon before the day is through. In the meantime, lay low and stay safe. I'm sure this will blow over."

"We'll talk soon," I said, unsure what else to offer.

I hung up, Sarah's face pinching tight with worry.

"Rehearsal is canceled," I said. "There are too many paps at the theatre. Alan sounds upset."

"He's not the only one," she sighed.

"Hey," I said, reaching over and pulling her into my arms. She fit so well there. "This will pass. The photographers will move on. We'll go back to life as scheduled."

"You're right," she said, leaning into me. "How long could it take, anyway?"

Sarah

I finally met Sergeant Pepper one week into our time at the Ritz. He was a monstrously fat old cat with a freaky level of intelligence in his gaze. Chris doted on him as if he were an infant and not a furry dictator, talking to him in a soft voice, offering him choices for each meal, taking any yowl back as an answer to his barrage of daily questions.

"I understand you prefer the pate, but we're down to the salmon in gravy until James gets back from the store."

Sgt. Pepper sat with a reverberating thump and yowled again, twitching his tail expectantly at Chris, who was leaned against the back of the sofa, legs crossed at the bare ankle. I watched from bed, a cup of coffee clutched in my hands, half-awake.

It had become our new routine: Chris would get up before me, do his movie star things like "eat breakfast" and "go to the gym" before returning with coffee and a plate of picture-perfect pastries from the Ritz member's lounge. Then he'd pad around the suite in his bare feet, sweatpants, and t-shirt, hair tousled from the shower, stubble turning into a full beard day-by-day.

My throat went dry as he bent to scoop wet food into Sgt. Pepper's bowl. The cat was in such a rush to suck down his breakfast that he was constantly shoving his head into the stream of gravy. While Chris lovingly wiped the stinky food from the cat's head, I tried not to drool over his sculpted ass thrust in the air, the way his toes gripped the carpet.

We'd been sharing a room for a week, and aside from the first night when he'd held me chastely for comfort, he hadn't so much as glanced in the direction of my bed.

Meanwhile, I was growing increasingly obsessed with his every intimate detail—the curl of leg hair surrounding his ankle bone, the crinkle in his cheeks when he laughed, the soft snort he let out every other breath when he slept.

If I wasn't careful, I was going to start sniffing his underwear.

I'd texted Angie about the sudden freeze in our blooming relationship and of course she'd texted back: "So jump him, tf?" Followed quickly by "Press is saying you're feisty and spicy. Prove it."

Personal hate for being called "spicy" aside, I couldn't take the lead. I was too scared of breaching the lines he'd drawn between us in our sudden hostage scenario. We couldn't go to our respective homes, couldn't go to the theatre, couldn't even leave the hotel for a change of scenery without getting mobbed. And despite being crushed together, I'd never felt further away from him.

Chris had immediately claimed the couch and let me have the bed—*alone*. In the last week, he'd spent most of his time running lines with Nicole on the phone and fielding manic voice messages from his agent, who apparently never graduated from using walkie-talkies.

"Will need your Hancock on a new agreement with the Nike people, over."

"Can't find your sides for DC project. Send stat. Over."

"New girl is cute, does she need rep? Over."

I'd winced at the last one, which Chris counted as a glowing review.

He'd shrugged when I asked him about it. "Steve's kind of an odd guy, but he gets me great work."

"Sarah?" I refocused my gaze on Chris' face as he straightened from feeding the cat. It was clear he'd said my name more than once, and my face burned bright as I silently prayed he wouldn't realize I'd been salivating over his ass.

"Sorry?"

"I was saying we could have a movie marathon today, since Nicole has that throat thing."

This was not enough information for me to act as if I'd been listening and had a momentary space-out. *Shit.*

"Sure." I hoped my smile was genuine and winning, not strained. But Chris squinted at me, arching an eyebrow.

"What's up?"

"Nothing." I tried to keep my voice light. "I'm down for a movie day if you are."

He settled on the end of the bed, a sea of white duvet between us.

"Look, I know this is weird, being cooped up all day with someone you just started seeing. If there's anything—"

"You're so far away." It came out before I could stop it, desire hauling the words across my teeth with a spine-shuddering scrape.

His mouth dropped into a slack "O," body twisting toward me as it landed with a soft *thwump* on top of the covers. He was *definitely not* far away now, his citrusy-clean smell wafting up to me. His hair was still damp from his morning shower and his beard looked soft and inviting on his chin as he looked up at me, head now only an inch from where my knee was wiggling under the blankets.

"I don't have to be," he said, voice low with something that made me want to rub against it like the cat.

Maybe we *had* been cooped up too long.

"Then why are you?" I gripped my coffee mug for dear life. All these pent-up feelings were doing a good job of smothering any fears that might try to rise. I wanted him to crawl on top of me, press me into the mattress, kiss me like he did the first time.

I wanted to disappear and never see him again.

I wanted to set my coffee down and straddle him, taking his face in both hands, wanted to feel his beard on the soft skin of my inner thigh.

"I worry about rushing you," he said. "I'm an all-in kinda guy."

I felt myself smile, a different kind of warmth in my chest than that which pooled quickly between my legs. "'All-in' like telling the entire theatre about us on the first day?"

He put his hands over his face and groaned. I'd been mocking him for a week, threatening to make him a t-shirt that said "Sarah Aguilar is My Girlfriend" in all capital letters ala Tom Hiddleston scaring off Taylor Swift. Too bad I wasn't interested in giving the paparazzi more fuel.

"Angie said she was proud of me for putting out so fast, so there's that at least." I laughed, polishing off the last of my coffee and avoiding his gaze. Usually, I moved at a glacial pace, notoriously breaking up with boyfriends that I'd seen for months and barely kissed twice.

I couldn't help that most men moving toward me with their mouths expectant made my entire body go ice cold and rigid. My palms would sweat, my heart would slam, and I'd squinch my face so uncomfortably would-be suitors backed off before they started.

Thanks again, Mr. Thompson.

"Did you tell her we—"

"*No!* No. Of course not. Cause we haven't—not yet. I mean, whenever we do is fine it's just she assumed that...you know cause you were so adamant about—"

"Fine?" He groaned again, hands still on his face.

"Or great! Better than fine! Probably amazing?" My voice was pitched up two octaves. I couldn't breathe. Maybe it was my turn to go to the gym and disappear for an hour. If not the gym, a portal to another dimension. The Ritz had that, right?

I wasn't a virgin, thank God. A few drunken nights in college had seen to that, with a plastic handle of vodka delivering a forgettable deflowering and a following hook-up that at least meant I knew how things worked.

"I'm so stupid." Chris muttered. Sitting up, taking his scent and warmth with him to the edge of the bed, I only had a split-second to mourn his distance before he was directly in front of me again, crawling across the bed like a tiger in grey sweatpants. He planted one hand on either side of my legs, bracing himself over my lap and looking up at me, barely inches away, but with enough distance I could easily escape.

If I wasn't frozen to the spot.

He radiated warmth, body ghosting over mine, breath landing on my neck and chin. "Sarah." He said my name like a plea, a prayer. It made my heart stutter, my blood swim thick and lazy in my body with a single wave of warmth. I shifted underneath him, finding the connection of brain to body, of heart to desire, that so often unplugged itself in moments like this. "I'm going to kiss you." I nodded, dumb, heart so loud I was sure he could hear it. "And then I'm going to fuck you until you know in your bones how close I want to be to you."

He took the coffee mug from my hands, setting it on the nightstand in an easy stretch that pressed him against me. Before he was done, my hands were skating over his beard, sinking into his hair, hauling his mouth to mine.

Any fears or hesitations I'd had were smothered under the electric heat sparking between us. He kissed me reverently, as if he couldn't believe it was happening—as if it were a wondrous event not likely to repeat. So, I kissed him back, again and again and again. I wanted him. I wanted him on me, around me, evaporated into particles so I could swim through him and feel his gentle kindness on my skin.

I gave in to all the horny thoughts I'd had all week, with him dancing just outside my reach, torturing me with his near-perfect smile, the shocking normalness of his movie star presence wrapped up in every-day clothes. As my fingers traced the shape of his throat, found the sensitive spot along his collar bone that made him gasp against my lips, I felt a certain power sing through me.

That gasp was in response to *me*. He was Captain Arrow Star, and he was practically trembling in front of me, hands flat against the mattress, following my lead, my pace, my needs.

I slid my hands further down, finding the hem of his shirt and tugging. He practically shot out of it, immediately readjusting to pull the white-T over his head with the speed of an eager teenager.

"I can't believe you're real," I whispered, a soft laugh gusting out of me at the sight of his tight abs, the sharp V of his waist disappearing into his clearly tented sweatpants.

"That's supposed to be my line," he whispered back, reconnecting our kiss with renewed need, nipping at my bottom lip, tongue pressing in. As I accepted it, he seemed to remember he had hands. He scooped me up against him, one hand firm on my ass in a possessive way that had me immediately wishing he'd arrange me in other, equally desirable positions. He kicked the duvet aside, laying me down with a gentle bounce on the pillows before settling between my legs. We groaned at the friction between us, his length hard against a delicious place. I ground against him, pulling at his hips, desperate to be closer, chasing sensation as something hot and desperate coiled at the base of my spine.

His mouth moved down my neck, hot and slow, teasing me as his hands slid under my shirt, tracing lines down my spine that arched me into the hard press of him.

Warning lights flashed in my brain.

No. Not now. Please not now.

The bugs returned, slamming across my skin hard and fast. I curled into myself, against my will, all the glorious warmth from Chris' touch vanished.

Please, not now.

I was here and I wasn't.

Too close. We were too close.

"Sarah?" He laid next to me, one hand propping up his head, the other by his side.

My voice wouldn't come, I already knew.

"You're so good, you know? Not like the others. No, my precious song-bird. You are so much better than them." His hand had a vise-like grip on my knee. I was frozen in fear, but something else, too—as if I felt obligated to wait for him to do whatever it was he planned. He'd taught me so much. He'd given me so many opportunities, lavishing me in attention. If I was the good girl he said I was, then I wouldn't punch his crooked teeth in for touching me.

"Sarah, look at me." Chris touched my cheek with the tips of his fingers, turning me toward him. His face interrupted the flashback, bright eyes dark with worry, mouth in a tight line. He swiped his thumb over each of my cheeks, and I realized I'd started crying.

I was not in the practice room at Concord Valley High. I was at the fucking Ritz in San Francisco, half-naked in bed with a movie star—a kind man who cared for me and *just* me.

"I'm sorry." I crumpled into a ball, as if I could pull myself into a tight-enough circle that the bugs wouldn't crawl on me, the past wouldn't suck me under.

"Don't apologize." Chris murmured. "Can I hold you?"

I nodded, chest and throat closed with the screaming sob I refused to release. But as his arms came around me, as he settled me gently against his body, pulling the duvet over us both, I was powerless against the cocoon of safety.

I cried like I'd meant to so long ago, helpless, exhausted, sad, terrified.

Heartbroken.

I cried like I'd always wanted to for myself, like I couldn't let anyone see when the college-ruled notes slid from hand to hand, when the whispers cascaded behind me like a venomous train on a dress I'd never wanted.

I mourned the optimistic girl I'd been then, fully believing I could sing my way to the stage I dreamed of, bolstered by my successes in the choir room. And I felt my heart break again for her as she dashed her own dreams on the hard rocks of an unfair world flipped against her.

And the whole time, tears making his bare chest sticky and wet, Chris held me, rubbing circles on my back, chin resting on top of my head.

Sometime later, wrung out and embarrassed, I swiped at my face then at his chest.

"I made a mess," I said.

"I don't mind." He loosened his hold on me as I sat up, pushing my hair away from my face and taking a deep, shuddering breath.

I don't know how long we sat there in silence. I didn't know what to say. I felt simultaneously apologetic and defensive. I didn't *need* to explain myself to anyone. But with Chris, I wanted to. I'd have been long gone by now with anyone else.

But I didn't exactly have anywhere to escape to. The thought had hot tears behind my eyes all over again, so I shoved it away.

"I'm sorry." He'd already said it was fine, don't apologize, it was okay. The same lines everyone always said, somehow shaped differently on his lips. When he told me it was okay, I believed him—maybe because it wasn't "I'm disappointed" wrapped in another package.

"You don't have to apologize," he said, stretching out in the bed. There again—he meant it.

"I think I do," I said, flopping my hands uselessly in my lap. "You give me your bed, sleep on the couch, lend me your security guards—"

"Because *I* brought the paparazzi to your theatre, Sarah. Don't think you had anything to do with that because it's out of our control." His voice was still soft but there was a firmness underpinning what he said. I turned to him, surprised at the backbone in this otherwise squishy man.

"You bring me coffee every morning and I can't even—"

"*Please.*" He held up a hand, cutting me off. "Please don't think you have to fuck me as a thank you."

I opened my mouth to protest, but quickly snapped it shut, mortified. I didn't think that, did I?

"If we make love," he started, and I couldn't stop my eyes from rolling at the phrase switch. He laughed, nudging me with his knee under the blanket. "Hey! I mean it! If we make love, it will be because we *both* want to and because we're *both* bonkers horny for each other. Not for any other reason. Ever."

I couldn't look at him, embarrassment and relief warring for dominance in my heart. But I laughed despite myself, feeling lightness return.

"Bonkers horny?" I glanced at him, shy.

"You heard me." He grinned at me as if I were the only star in a darkening sky. I didn't deserve it, and I suddenly couldn't stand his attention.

I excused myself to shower and get a grip, locking the door behind me. I ran the water, waiting for it to warm out of habit—I was sure his water always arrived hot—and let myself sink to the tiled floor.

What now?

SARAH

"It happened again." I didn't have to text anything else before Angie was a flurry of rapid responses.

"OMG"

"No, girl."

"I'm so sorry. Are you okay?"

"How did Chris respond? I'll kill him, I stg."

"He was perfect, of course." I texted back. "He promised the only way we'd hook up was if we were both 'bonkers horny' for each other."

Angie sent the cry-laughing emojis in a long string.

"He did not say that wtf."

Three little dots danced on the screen as the bathroom grew steamy. I left my phone on the counter, quickly tucking my hair into a shower cap and shedding my pajamas. I braced myself against the cool tile wall, letting the scorching water slam into my chest, thundering through me and chasing the bugs out from under my skin.

I knew what Angie would ask next. It was what she always asked when I talked with her about these frozen flashbacks.

Will you tell him?

Of all the past candidates, Chris at least seemed like he'd be receptive to my baggage. But I wasn't sure I could bring myself to add to my list of cons. I already felt like I was standing on the doorstep of his life, surrounded by piles marked WRONG—I made barely any money, I wasn't an actor never mind working in movies, I lived in the wrong city for him, and now I was also that girl who froze up during sex.

I was sure any headline would agree, but as I emerged from my steamy cocoon, some self-sabotaging part of me couldn't resist confirming. Swiping away from my conversation with Angie, I typed in Chris' name to search.

There was the racist reference to my spiciness that Angie had mentioned—why was it only Latina women that earned that adjective? I scrolled past, letting my eyes linger on pictures of Chris and me holding hands, walking down the street, leaving the theatre. I looked so happy, I barely recognized myself. And Chris—I blushed at the look on his face, the soft way he gazed at me, the warmth in his smile.

We looked perfect.

The photo carousel had a comment section, and I should've known better than to peek. Any joy I'd felt at the photos evaporated.

"Fat."

"Not fair!"

"Why is he with an UGGO!!!!"

There were several comments in a row that said such blatantly racist things I sped past them, as if I could dodge the attack by refusing to acknowledge it.

"There goes my chance!"

"This is what's wrong with this country. A beautiful American man with an illegal—"

I slammed the phone down on the bathroom counter. That was enough of that.

Any waffling I'd had disappeared. It was clear that all I could do was peer in at Chris' glamorous life from the outside. I'd never be invited in without him needing to defend me from every accusatory whisper.

No. I wouldn't tell him.

In fact, it would be best to have a clean break now before anything else happened. We could continue camping out—or I could find somewhere else to crash until things blew over.

Resolved, I turned off the shower and slid into a robe that felt more like a fluffy cloud than terry cloth. I felt firmer on the ground, now the bugs had been burned away, now I was back at the controls of my own body.

But all my intentions vanished at Angie's next text, pinging from beneath my hand like the death-rattle of a helpful ladybug.

"How are you practicing self-care?"

"And I don't mean packing your shit and running away because things got intimate and vulnerable."

I let out a frustrated sigh, raspberrying my lips in the mirror. *This bitch.*

"Damn girl, way to read me to filth," I texted back.

I could practically see her crossing her arms and tapping her foot. Angie was a die-hard social media therapist devotee, with several cropping up in her daily feed. Sometimes she'd send them to me, and I'd half-listen to their 90 second pitch on CPTSD, parentification, and the big 4 Fs: fight, flight, freeze, and fawn. Her messages were often the only reason I opened the apps—although my new celebrity boyfriend might have my empty page blowing up.

"Well?" Angie pinged again. "Self-care" and "self-compassion" were her latest fixations, manifesting as regular nail appointments, a card catalogue of face masks, and a stack of Chinese poetry she told me she read in the sunniest patch of her apartment like a cat enjoying a sleepy afternoon.

As her own regimen developed, she turned her attention to me, in her signature, overbearing, obsessive Angie way. She dropped an entire box of face masks off one night, chattering about when to use each kind. Books on meditation and journaling for reflection started piling up in the mail room, as if she'd only thought to send each one as she found them online. The final straw was a gift-wrapped jar of bougie bath salts for the bathtub I don't have.

But still, Angie persisted in her caring crusade, asking for regular check-ins on my self-care strategies and plans. The most I'd managed was "listening to my body," which I did explain to her meant slamming a bag of Takis in bed watching *On My Block* for the fifth time.

"You know I'm bad at this." I didn't have time to elaborate or excuse before she texted back.

"What would feel good right now?"

Disappearing. Teleporting to another country. But then I thought about the oceanic duvet right outside the bathroom door, fluffy and cool, but just the right weight to send me off to sleep with minimal tossing and turning. I thought about the hot tea and cookies Chris ordered us from room service a few nights prior, the mug warm in my hands, the cookies filling the room with a pleasant, sugary scent long after we'd devoured them.

"Well, first I have to break up with Chris. And then I think I'm going to order room service."

My phone rang immediately.

"Angie I can't—"

"*Are you actually insane?*"

I held the phone away from my ear, hyper aware of how her voice echoed in the bathroom despite not being on speaker.

"Can you shut the fuck up? I've already been in the bathroom for way too long, I don't need him to hear me talking to you," I hissed. "People think I'm some greedy cartoon character running off with their treasured Mr. America. They called me *spicy*."

"*I don't give a fuck! Breaking up with* the *Chris Smolders because why? He was* nice *to you?*"

"You know it's not like that."

"Do I?" She stopped yelling for a moment, but I could hear her breath coming hard through the phone. "I've always supported you when it comes to this. You know that. And the last guys deserved it—I mean who asks for a blow job after their date freaks out mid-make out session?"

Jamie did.

"And what kind of sociopath insists you don't have it 'that bad' because you haven't killed yourself yet?"

That was Paulo.

"Tell me what he said."

I sighed. "I did already."

"Say it."

I turned my back on the door, cupping my hand against phone as if I could muffle my voice.

"If we make love, it will be because we both want to and because we're both bonkers horny for each other."

"Are you fucking serious." It wasn't a question so much as a lengthy expletive when she said it that way.

"Deadly."

Angie sighed, breath coming as static through the phone.

"Look. Do what you want. I can't force you. But maybe think about what it could look like to be with someone who holds every part of you, not just the parts that are convenient."

I was silent. She took the opening.

"Because you've never done that before."

I hadn't.

"I hate you." I didn't.

"Not as much as I hate you." She didn't either.

A soft knock at the bathroom door interrupted our clandestine phone call.

"I have to go," I whispered. I heard her making kissing sounds into the phone as I tapped the END button.

"Sarah?" Chris' voice came through the door.

I opened it in a whoosh of steamy air, completely forgetting I was still wearing my shower cap and robe.

Chris had added a hoody to match his sweatpants but otherwise looked unchanged. There was still a pinch of worry between his brows, blue eyes soft as they took me in, hands immediately cupping my elbows, holding me.

I wasn't going to break up with him.

"How are you doing?"

"Better," I said, fidgeting with the cuff of the robe. "Nothing a hot shower can't fix."

"And a chat with Angie." His mouth twitched up at the corners.

My hands flew up to cover my face as I blushed down to my feet.

"How much did you hear?" I asked through my fingers.

"None of it, I swear. I would never eavesdrop on your bathroom time."

"Then how did you—"

He dug into his hoody pocket, pulling out his phone where a barrage of all-caps texts from an unknown number were still pinging across his screen.

"Ah." I grabbed his phone, a slow smile breaking into full-on laughter as I read her messages.

"My favorite is the one that compares my career to a careening, violent meteor meant to burn out before reaching its full potential but not before obliterating anyone in its path."

"That's mean," I paused, glancing at his bemused face. "But poetic." I was okay with Angie defending my honor. In fact, I kind of liked it. "I told her the truth, by the way. She's just got a quick fuse."

"I'm glad you have her in your corner," he said. "Because being on the receiving end of her wrath is confusingly inspiring and scary."

"Did I tell you she eventually wants to be a playwright?" I was dissolved into giggles now, handing his phone back, leaning against the door frame for support.

"Great. I'm honored to contribute material for..." he scrolled up on his phone. "Captain Arrow Star More Like Major Fart Bitch by Angie Chen."

We were both laughing now, and I couldn't help but notice how his body shifted, shoulders relaxing and stretching wide from their hunch, hips swaying naturally with his joy.

Catching his breath, he gestured toward the sofa and TV, just out of sight from where I hadn't fully emerged from the bathroom.

"Whenever you're ready, I got some help setting up our movie marathon."

I glanced at him in confusion then followed his gaze to where my robe was beginning to gap open.

We both blushed simultaneously—he cleared his throat and looked away, I slid back into the bathroom, ducking behind the half-open door.

"Just a minute." I gritted out, closing the door the rest of the way.

Getting back into my pajamas, I mouthed all the silent, mortified screams I needed to get it out of my system. Then, taking off the shower cap and tousling my curls until I was satisfied, I gave the mirror my best square-shouldered, chin-up, we-can-do-this stare.

Maybe I *could* let someone hold all of me. Not today, but someday.

For now, there was about to be some serious cuddling in my future and that sounded like the best self-care I could ask for.

When I finally left my tiled fortress, I felt like a new person re-entering the suite. I felt stronger, surer, renewed in a way that a shower alone couldn't accomplish. Although Chris and I hadn't talked about our interruption directly, Angie had united us better than she knew. Chris could handle crazy, judging by his bemused but laughing response to her threats. What was a little teenage trauma in comparison?

Chris was waiting for me, arms spread wide like Vanna White at the letter board, gesturing to an entire cozy fort he'd apparently had time to setup while I was making other plans.

Extra blankets and pillows created a soft, fluffy nest out of the formerly formal sofa. Twinkle lights hung from the ceiling and winked from around the TV. A room service cart was parked at the edge of the hygge oasis, wafting the familiar smell of cookies and something else, hot and sugary.

"I think you might be a mind reader." I leapt over the sofa, snuggling down into the blankets with a happy purr.

He filled two mugs, handing me one with a strange look on his face as I practically screamed with joy.

"Hot coco!" It was so sweet my teeth hurt, and it was definitely missing the cinnamon and chile Mami added to hers, but it did its job, spreading warmth across my chest as I settled back into my seat.

Chris joined me, carefully watching his cup as he slid under the blanket, lifted my legs onto his lap, and pulled me under the crook of his arm.

"Should we start with Arnold or Salma?"

We'd had a moment of mutual disbelief when I mentioned never seeing any *Terminator* movies, and he'd shared he didn't know anything about *Desperado*.

Obviously, the only solution to our individual lacking was to watch the movies together. But I hadn't imagined he'd put so much thought into making it feel special.

"Hey," I nudged his leg with my toe, getting his attention from where he was flipping through the different streaming services. "Is this a date?"

He shook his head, and my heart plummeted.

Gently moving my legs from his lap and sitting up straighter, he pulled me into a sitting position next to him.

Oh.

We sat that way for a stunned moment before Chris let out an over-exaggerated yawn, stretching his arms above his head before letting one drop with a comedic flop onto my shoulders.

"Now it's a date." He kissed my forehead, clearly pleased with himself, before clicking on *Terminator*. The movie intro started, and I sipped my coco, leaning my head on Chris' shoulder as his thumb traced lazy circles on my arm.

This could be good.

Maybe even great.

CHRIS

Three weeks in, I couldn't stand to look at the hotel anymore. I called James and Greg to ask them to be on duty that night, texted Jess and asked her to make a dinner reservation, and then I did something risky.

Glancing at Sarah, her head of curls bent over her stage notebook, extra pages spread out across the bed in an arc around her. She'd given Jess her apartment keys in week one of our hideout stay, guiding her over the phone to which clothing was stored where and what she'd need to be comfortable. But, of course, she hadn't planned for a fancy dinner date. I worried she'd feel self-conscious wearing jeans to the restaurant, but then again it *was* San Francisco. The city was notorious for men in fleece zip-ups appearing in all sorts of high-end venues and refusing to so much as lace up their New Balances.

Maybe I could admit the truth to myself—that I wanted to spoil Sarah a little, that I wanted to gift her an evening straight out of a romantic comedy.

I gave in to the urge and texted Jess again, this time with a photo of Sarah I'd taken at the rooftop bar of the hotel. She was smiling at me, chin jutting forward, curls wild in the wind, a blood-red sunset against the city skyline behind her.

"Can you get a dress and shoes for Sarah for dinner tonight? It's a surprise so I can't ask her size…"

"Challenge accepted." Jess texted back immediately with the thumbs-up emoji. Not for the first time, I was grateful for my assistant and even more pleased I'd taken a chance on a sandwich artist who wanted to make the leap into the world of personal assistants. She'd needed no training and answered my every ask with prompt delivery, regardless of the lengths she went to get it.

I was nothing without her.

"Good thing I've already rifled through her closet, I can figure it out." She followed up.

Now I just had to ask Sarah out.

We'd spent the last three weeks together, cooped up and coping as more and more tabloid headlines screamed online and outside. Now I was running a cult of sexy PAs that I'd recruited throughout my career, although who they were and what I wanted with them remained a mystery—I was thankful no one was taking the bait and there remained no "cult" members to exclusively interview.

I wiped my sweating palms on my pantleg and took a deep breath.

"Would you go to dinner with me tonight?"

Sarah's head whipped up from her notebook, eyes wide, jaw slack. Three weeks together and I was still obsessed with the crunch of her nose, the wispy tendrils of curls that clung to her face, the way her hands fidgeted with the duvet when I asked her a direct question like right now.

"Like, out-out?" She gestured toward the window where we'd finally opened the curtains to let in rare sunshine.

I nodded solemnly. "Out-out."

"Is that a good idea?"

"No. Absolutely not."

Her shoulders slumped.

"But we're doing it anyway."

She smiled, dimpled cheeks making my heart flutter.

"Where do you want to go? There's this incredible taquería on Mission, or Chinatown is super close, we could walk over and find what's open. Ooo and we could get egg tarts after—"

"I was actually thinking I'd take you someplace nice." Her mouth slammed shut and she straightened, crossing her arms. I realized too late my mistake, flashing back to our first dinner together in the Chinese restaurant. She didn't want to be taken care of—in fact she seemed to fight it aggressively.

"I probably can't afford anywhere you'd want to go."

"That's why I'm covering it."

"No, that's too much. I can't—"

"Sarah, please." I clasped my hands together like I had the first time. "Please let me do this."

"Why?"

"Because I want to. Because I luh—AHEM—like you."

Her eyebrows disappeared into her hairline as she shot me a look.

"Because it's fun for me to take people I like to a nice meal, and because if I have to stare at this room anymore, I'm going to fucking lose it."

Sarah closed her notebook.

"How nice?"

"Alexander's."

"Chris, no. I don't have anything to wear to a place like that."

"I may have already taken care of that too." I pressed my steepled fingers to my lips, bracing myself for her response.

"Are you Pretty Womaning me?"

"I think you have to be a sex worker for that to apply."

"But you're dressing me up and putting me on display."

"You don't have to wear the dress, but I thought it'd be nice for you to have the option."

"Cause what I own isn't nice enough for the places you like to go."

"Sarah, stop. Go to dinner with me."

"If I say no?"

I sighed, frustrated. This woman was going to be the death of me. I needed back up. I tapped my phone a few times, lifting it to my ear as it rang.

"What are you doing?" Her voice pitched up an octave. I didn't love the fear I heard in it.

"Carl Mercer's Mortuary Speed Dating Hotline, they say 'over my dead body' and we say 'where?'"

I glanced at the screen, double checking the number I'd dialed. I heard Angie's voice cackling through the line.

"Gotcha, bitch."

"Hi, Angie. Look, I won't keep you, but I'm thinking of taking Sarah to Alexander's." I pulled the phone away from my ear a second time as she shrieked.

"Oh my god? Oh my *god-uh*. Chris she's gonna die."

"She's gonna die?" I repeated, glancing meaningfully at Sarah who was now beet red and glaring at me. "And what would you say if I told you she was refusing to go?"

The line was silent a moment.

"Give her the phone," she said in a voice I imagined coming from Liam Neeson in an action franchise and not a 5-foot curvy East Asian woman.

"Someone wants to yell at you," I said, smugly handing Sarah the phone. It was received with an eye roll. I smothered a laugh as Sarah immediately launched the phone a foot from her face. Angie's screaming voice chattered on about chances, and self-care, and I think I heard something about someone holding her. I wasn't sure what that last part meant, but whatever it was, it got through to Sarah.

"Fine! I'll go. Jesus fucking Christ."

Sarah thrust the phone back at me.

"Thank you, Angie." I made a smooching noise into the phone like I'd heard her and Sarah do so many times over the last three weeks.

"Do you think you're clever?" But Sarah was grinning, ear-to-ear, lifting herself off the bed and striding toward me in a way that made me cough while I adjusted myself through my pants.

"I *may* have been told that before, yes." I returned her smile as she draped her arms around my shoulders, pressing herself against me.

"I'm supposed to say thank you for taking me to dinner and thank you for the dress." She murmured, words dancing across my lips and enticing my tongue out to taste them.

"And?" I gave in, grabbing her by the hips and letting my hands wander. Ever since her panic attack the last time, we'd been taking things slow and chaste—kissing, cuddling, touching. But nothing explicit. And I would wait until the end of time if it meant she felt safe with me.

But man, as soon as she was ready, the minute I got an invitation, I was going to worship every enticing curve on her body, every decadent slice of skin—as if she were my last meal and I was condemned to death row.

"We'll see." She kissed me, just once, before twirling out of reach and sashaying into the shower.

I held my glass of champagne out across the table, not caring about the cheesy grin plastered on my face as Sarah's class clinked against mine. She took a small sip, turning to gaze out the floor-to-ceiling windows surrounding us, the glittering city sprawled out in all directions. I watched her throat bob as she swallowed, trying to memorize the lines of her in the candlelight.

The dining room was an elegant sea of cloth napkins and white tablecloths, where people murmured to one another across delicate bouquets nestled against tealights, the only other sound the light scrape of cutlery on fine china.

Jess had found Sarah a deep maroon, knee-length dress that fell off her shoulders. The dramatic rouching across the chest drew the eye to all her curves and when she walked, the skirts swung around her legs with a quiet whispering of chiffon. I could easily imagine her on the red carpet, hand tucked through my arm, smiling demurely for the cameras.

I'd chosen my favorite suit—tailored, black, single button—and Jess had grabbed me a silk shirt to match Sarah's dress. It was a little prom-esque, I know, but I didn't care. It was clearly a good move, since I caught Sarah's eyes roaming over my chest more than once, heating me all over and making me wish there was somewhere more discrete we could slip away to.

Sarah giggled as she lifted her glass to her nose. "It tickles," she said, before her attention was stolen by yet another steaming dish passing us by.

"I need to take you out more," I said, leaning my chin in my hand. "This is fun."

"Enjoy it while it lasts," she said. "Alan thinks we'll be able to get back to work soon. This might be our first and last night out for a while."

"We'll always have Mondays," I said with the same dramatic flair that other romantic leads would give to "we'll always have Paris."

She laughed, a little louder than anyone around us, and I drank it in, ignoring the few stares.

"Sorry," She whispered, face flushed from the alcohol.

"Don't be," I said. "Everyone else should laugh a little louder in general. Especially you."

She set her champagne down, a solemn look on her face as she cocked her head to the side. Her fingers toyed with stem of the glass, twisting it one way then another.

"Why do you say things like that?"

"Like what?"

"Like, telling me people should laugh like me. Or that you'd listen to me through every door in the city if you had to." She flushed through her cheeks to her neck, dusting her chest the same delicious color.

"Because it's true."

Sarah rolled her eyes, arched a dark eyebrow, pushed a curl behind her ear. God, I wanted to drink her out of the air in front of me, swallow her whole, never breathe again for fear of exhaling her too quickly.

"People don't just say shit like that," she said quietly.

"What are you implying? I'm an alien?"

"Yeah," she grinned down at her lap. "You must be."

"I don't think saying what I mean qualifies me as an ET."

"It might."

I reached across the table, prying her fidgeting fingers from the glass and wrapping them in my hands. Her skin was soft and warm, and I let my fingers trace over it.

"I'm excited about you Sarah. And I know that probably comes off as *a lot*, but I came to San Francisco feeling more lost and alone than I have in my life. And here you were, slamming pap mics in iron doors and leading me around the city like a secret agent."

"Anyone would've done that."

"No, they wouldn't." It came out firmer than I'd meant, but I couldn't help the heat that jolted through me as she straightened in her seat. *Filing that away for later.*

Sarah laced her fingers through mine, leaning forward over the table.

"I'm excited about you, too," she practically whispered. "And it's really scary for me." Her eyes were wet, her bottom lip trembling. I wished there was something I could do to—

"Madame," the waiter appeared at Sarah's elbow, and she gave a throttled yelp. "Your filet mignon, rare, with whipped potatoes and our seasonal oven-roasted offering."

"Sir, your ribeye with peppercorn, baked potato, and broccolini." As soon as he set the plate down in front of me, my stomach roared to life. We waited until the waiter bid us a "bon appetite," before slicing into our meals in silence. The knife bit through my steak easily, and I closed my eyes around the first bite. It was juicy, tender, flavorful. I might never do another movie again if it meant I could eat like this more than once a year.

The thought crystalized, hovered, pulling my focus from the moment.

What *if* I lived like this for a while? Doing live theatre, enjoying San Francisco, exploring my relationship with Sarah. I had enough money put away I wouldn't need to return to LA for a long time. Hell, I could move to San Francisco if I really wanted to.

Move to San Francisco.

That was too much to chew on while my mouth was full of steak.

SARAH

"You know you probably can't ask Alan to close his eyes while you audition." Chris' voice floated over the back of the sofa where he was settling, resting his hands behind his head so I had a good view of his thick biceps.

I'm going to lick them when we're done here, bugs be damned.

With all the chaos at the theatre finally slowing down, Alan had called to schedule my audition, giving me an extra week to prepare than I had planned for. I'd been getting up in the morning with Chris, using the hour he was at the gym to practice in the empty hotel room.

Every day was charged with anticipation as the audition crept closer, my heart a dangerous cocktail of excitement, fear, and something else that grew between me and Chris, intertwining us deeper.

It was that something that prompted me to stop him from going to the gym that morning. I pulled up the memory of us at karaoke together—the first night we'd kissed, but also the first time I'd not asked for a lack of eyes when I sang. I'd felt brave then, when Chris locked eyes with me on stage, and I needed that bravery to return.

But when Chris settled in front of me in the hotel room we'd started calling "home," my blood ran cold. I didn't even make it through the opening lines before slamming the power button on the Bluetooth speaker.

"I'll burn that bridge when I get to it," I said, pressing my hands flat against my chest and stomach, feeling their weight, coming into my breath and my body.

I'd decided to stick with my song—the one that had siren called Chris through our thin walls. "Back to Before" wasn't a hugely popular choice, which meant Alan's eyes wouldn't glaze over when I started. And I already knew I could sing the hell out of it. Angie loved how I sang "Being Alive," but I wasn't about to audition for a show with material from itself.

"When you're ready, Miss Aguilar." Chris mimicked Alan's voice from over the sofa. I rolled my eyes to suppress the laughter bubbling up. He was going to ruin my character before I got into it.

The melodic intro was far too short before my voice joined in.

Although "Mother"—no, really, that's her name—in *Ragtime* is bemoaning how the old ways can't be replicated in a more modern era, to me the song was about being brave enough to leave the known world behind. A controlled world reliant on the structure imposed by her husband. Or, in my case, a world held hostage by Mr. Thompson.

I'd never been a socialite housewife at the turn of the century, but I knew the uncertainty of stepping forward with no plotted course. I knew what it was to be guided so surely, so safely to new shores only to be abandoned—unmoored.

And as the bridge entered, shifting keys, Mother's marveling at braver people than her became motivation for me. If others could be unafraid of tomorrow or of being wrong, then I could, too. I could face the new world laid out before me with courage.

In the final stanza, I let my voice break free with the swell of the orchestra, let the final words ring across the room and up to the ceiling as I repeated that we could never go "back to before." It was a promise to myself—a refusal to return to the past that so often threatened to drag me out of the present.

By the time I finished, Chris had turned around against my instructions and was watching me with an intensity in his gaze that pooled heat between my legs, my stomach flipping repeatedly.

I tapped the speaker off before the song could repeat—a habit from Pine Street life I realized didn't need to carry over to the Ritz. I felt divided, split between experiences, straddling worlds. All because of a single button.

"Your voice is a gift. Every time." Chris murmured, resting his chin on the back of the sofa.

"I don't know if I can do this." I was shaking now, confusion wiping away any warmth or desire I'd felt only moments ago. I'd done it—I'd sang full-throttle in front of a man in a closed room. A man I trusted. A man like Alan.

And I was safe. So, so safe.

The room tilted and I let my legs fold under me, half-falling, half-sitting on the floor.

"Sarah?" Chris' voice came from somewhere far away, edged with concern and something else I couldn't name.

"Word to the wise, Sarah," Liv readjusted her grip on her textbook and binder, pressing them close to her chest. "I don't think every Broadway star fucked their choir teacher. You might want to reconsider your strategy."

She was gone before I could defend myself, leaving me dumbstruck and mortified in a completely silent school hallway. Everyone was look-

ing at me. Even a few teachers stuck their heads out of their classrooms to see what kind of chaos was happening.

"Alright, everyone to your classes, no lingering." The voice froze me to the spot. I was abandoned as my classmates scurried away, heads down, to their classes. Doors swung shut, and the muffled sounds of life as usual leaked through cracks and windows.

"Sarah." I turned, as if directed by a puppet master, my head, neck, limbs not my own. "You'll see me in my office." I nodded, dumb, and followed in his footsteps. I was supposed to be in Geometry, but Mr. Thompson would give me a note.

He always did.

"Sarah."

He closed the door behind me, the metal thud more like a jail cell slamming shut than a choir room entry.

"I've been hearing some disturbing rumors going around." He crossed his arms, leveling a glare at me from over his round, wire-frame glasses. He'd shaved his usual mustache, and I hated how tiny it made his mouth look—as if such a miniscule thing couldn't possibly be harmless. All it did was make me think of poisonous frogs, killing predators with a single touch.

"Do you have anything to say for yourself?"

I stared, unsure how to respond. I hadn't started rumors about myself, especially not something so nasty. Did he think I had? Was he expecting an apology?

"Well, if you remain tight-lipped, I'm afraid I'll have to take action to protect myself. I've already been asked to Mrs. Jone's office this afternoon. They take rumors more seriously than proof, these days."

"I didn't say anything." I couldn't look at him. His gaze pinned me in place, held me there when every nerve in my body was screaming to run.

"About what? There wasn't anything for you to say." He snapped. "Nothing. Happened."

Then why was he so angry? What did he think he needed to protect?

Mr. Thompson leaned back against his desk, letting silence hang heavy in the air. Finally, with an aggravated sigh, he continued.

"Gwen is taking the first solo for competition." I felt my heart snap, an ache so painful I needed to hold a hand to my chest to soothe it. But I wouldn't let him see he'd won. So, I waited. "I can't have anyone claiming favoritism, not with your nastiness running around the school now. Do you realize I could get fired?"

My nastiness.

"Sarah, you're okay." Chris' voice cut through the flashback, superimposing his face, his worried eyes, the swoop of blond hair, overtop the vivid, painful memory. Reaching for him felt like swimming through Jello, my limbs heavy and exhausted. I let him cradle me, pulling me into his lap on the floor and running soothing hands over my back, my face, pushing my hair from my eyes.

This time, I let myself cry, let the grief sweep through me, as one thought played over and over and over again.

I was just a kid.

Finally, when I'd caught my breath and the hotel room was back in focus, firmly in reality, Chris tilted my face, meeting my eyes.

"Will you talk about it with me?"

I nodded, and before I lost my courage or my comfort, I let the story pour out of me. All of it: how much I'd loved singing in high school, the lessons with Mr. Thompson, how they turned strange and possessive, *that* day, and the mess after.

When I was done, he was silent, his mouth a thin line.

"I'm—"

"Please." Chris cut me off, pressing me harder against him. "Please don't apologize, Sarah."

I nodded, letting myself nuzzle into his chest, inhaling the bright smell of him.

"Okay." I let loose a shuddering breath. I felt lighter, somehow, as if I'd been carrying twenty pounds around for some mysterious errand and I'd only just realized there was no point in clutching to it so tightly. I *could* set it down.

"Can I ask you a question?" Taking my face in both his hands, I felt cherished and protected, as if nothing bad could ever happen to me again.

"Are you in therapy?"

I shook my head. "That's for rich people," I said, trying to joke but hearing it fall slat in the tension. I swiped at my eyes, moving away from Chris' touch.

"It's not. It's for everyone."

"My insurance doesn't cover it, and all the free places are backed up for months. It's not worth the trouble."

"It could be. Sarah, I think you have trauma over what happened to you with that perverted prick." He spit out the accidental alliterative insult with such venom, I felt my heart clench. I imagined him punching Mr. Thompson into a bloody pulp while wearing the Captain Arrow Star outfit.

"Why are you smiling at me?"

I shook my head. We could revisit that later.

"Trauma is for other people." I slammed a hand over my mouth, startled at Mami's words coming out of me.

Chris shook his head but let me sit with my own thoughts for the moment. After the silence felt so present, I thought about asking it to speak, he finally broke it.

"You are a gift of a woman, and a talented singer. I hope you'll let yourself heal the way you deserve. When you're ready." He stood, offering his hand to pull me up with him.

I let him, because the carpet was pebbling my knees, and because all he'd ever done in our time together was lift me to his level, sweeping everything else out from under me but securing me by his side, never letting me stumble.

"I'll look into it."

Chris pressed a kiss to my temple, then whispered, "But first, lunch."

Chris

It had been weeks since I arrived in San Francisco that first day, following Sarah with hearts in my eyes to my new old front door. It had been more days than I cared to count since I had fiddled with my keys, trying to draw out more of her time before we closed our doors to one another.

And still, standing in the hallway again, free of our glamorous cage at the Ritz, everything felt brand new. It was as if we'd never been here, as if we hadn't done this part before.

"Can't wait to sleep in my own bed." Sarah shrugged one shoulder, her keys dangling off a crooked finger.

"I'd say 'same,' but..." *But I want to sleep next to you.* I bit off the rest of the thought. I was finally striking a good balance in this flight-risk two-step we were doing around each other. Sarah was holding a lot—only some of which I'd come to understand—and I couldn't shake the feeling she'd bolt if I told her how I truly felt.

I'd probably run away from me. It was too much, too soon, too fast. But that didn't make it any less real.

"Are you nervous at all? About your promo interview?" She asked, eyes looking anywhere but me. I had a video call with a late-night host in New York to promote *Caught Red-Handed*. My agent mentioned the host wanted to talk about my stepping away from Hollywood more than the play, but I'd still get the chance for a promo plug.

I shook my head. "It'll be easy."

Silence stretched between us. I couldn't stand it. But I didn't want it to end.

The end meant she'd go in her door. I'd go in mine.

"Is it weird?" Sarah nodded toward my door. I knew from the change in her tone, the way she shifted from foot-to-foot, that she wasn't talking about the promo anymore. Was it weird staying in the same apartment I'd grown up in? The one my mom had nearly died in? The apartment that was and was not still mine?

"Super weird, yeah." *Why lie?*

Her face fell, and I didn't miss the guilt that flashed across it.

That's why. Lie better next time.

"But it's a weird I need. Remember I paid money for the weird." Sarah closed the gap between us, looping a sure arm around my waist and kissing me softly. I could've sworn I heard a symphony in the background.

"I'm only three feet away if you need me."

I cupped her face in my hands, feeling the rightness of it—her cheeks settled in my palms as if they'd been molded together, the softness of her, the smell of her shampoo, all combining to wind me tighter and tighter around that same finger dangling her keys.

"I need you." I kissed her, feeling her laugh against my mouth.

"You know what I mean." She swatted at me, but I didn't let go, kissing her again. This time it was steady, deep, as if I could drink her in to tide me over through the long, lonely night. She let out a quiet moan, parting her lips to me, tilting her head up, and I felt something unleash. I slid my hands along the base of her scalp, digging my fingers into those thick, gorgeous curls and tugging lightly. I heard her keys drop but I didn't stop, hauling Sarah against me, desperate for every curve of her.

Her hands found my hips, slipping under the hem of my shirt and jacket, soft palms skating across my back. When I kissed her this time, her nails dug in lightly, shooting heat to my core where I already felt it threatening to erupt.

"Come inside with me," I pleaded against her mouth, pulling away just enough to search her deep brown eyes for hesitation. There was none as she nodded, dipping down to get her keys and looping an arm through her worn duffel in the same motion.

My hands shook as I tried to slot the key in, my heart slamming in my chest, pulse roaring in my ears. *This* was why no one could open doors in horror movies—adrenaline was a bitch.

Sarah's hands closed over mine, guiding the key into the lock, turning it with more confidence than I felt. She pressed against me, muscling me against the door as she turned the knob. I felt it lift slightly as she did so, and I was struck by her hidden strength.

"She stronk." I wanted to melt into the floor at my stupid, *stupid* joke as the door swung open. But Sarah giggled, smacking me on the shoulder.

"Don't ruin the mood." She grabbed me by the jacket, giving me barely enough time to catch my suitcase as she hauled me into the apartment, slamming the door shut behind us.

Sarah pressed me into the door, kissing me like she could melt me into the wood with her mouth—at this rate, she probably could. I let her take the lead, lacing our fingers together and guiding my hands above my head. Pinned like an audience member in a throwing knife act, it was all I could do to grind against Sarah through my punishing jeans. My body was screaming for friction, overpowering any other need in my mind.

Another laugh ghosted over my mouth as Sarah released one of my hands only to glide hers between us, gripping my cock through the denim. I slammed my head against the door, thrusting into her touch. I nearly cried when she undid the fly and zipper, dropping to her knees to put both hands on me.

"God, please, Sarah." I didn't know who I was praying to—the big guy or her clever fingers as they worked me out of my boxers.

"I wasn't going to come in here," Sarah purred, pushing my pants further down my hips. "I really was looking forward to my bed. But then I realized…" She fisted the base of my cock and ran a teasing tongue under my length. Every other muscle in my body clenched. "I wouldn't hear your cute little snore tonight." She licked me from base to tip again, this time laving just beneath the head. Stars were bursting in the corner of my eyes.

"Sarah, I'm gonna—"

"No, you aren't. Because I'm not done with you." *Fuck, that was hot.* "And you're such a good, kind, caring man. You won't disappoint me." She took me entirely in her mouth then, sucking perfectly so that her cheeks hollowed. I was at her mercy, unable to stop myself from fucking her face as she worked me with her gorgeous, wet lips and tongue, palming my balls with just enough pressure to make me cry out but not enough to release me from this beautiful torture.

"Fuck, Sarah—" I reached for her, barely touching the back of her head before her free hand slammed against mine, pressing it against the door. She released my cock with a wet pop of her lips.

"Hands flat," she said, pressing my other hand back until it mirrored the first.

"That's not fair." I couldn't touch her? Couldn't feel her body this close to mine?

"Life's not fair." There was an edge in her voice that shocked me, but I barely had time to turn it over in my mind before she returned to my cock, sucking me harder, faster, than before.

I was gone, fucking her mouth in sharp, rhythmic thrusts, palms slick with sweat against the door as I scrambled to stay upright. Everything disappeared, my heart and soul tunneled to just the pinpoint of light that was Sarah's mouth, hauling me to the edge of orgasm before throwing me over it with an inexplicable twisting in one place and sucking in another.

I tried to pull out and come in my hand, but Sarah pushed back against my hips, swatting at my hands as she took my hot release down the back of her throat.

Sgt. Pepper decided right then was when he'd ask for dinner, streaking past us into the kitchen with a shrieking yowl. Sarah and I stared at each other, breathless, her chest heaving through her t-shirt in a way that was already making my dick twitch again.

"Aye, aye captain." She said, wiping delicately at the edge of her lips before standing and breezing by me into the kitchen. She barely had a can of cat food in her capable hands before I grabbed her by the waist, lifting her easily and throwing her over my shoulder. She shrieked, kicking her feet in the air.

"Chris! Put me down!"

It was three quick strides to the bedroom from the kitchen, a distance that once felt so much bigger, a long, long time ago. I shoved the thought aside, dropping Sarah with a delicious bounce on the bed.

"Put you down." I grinned, crawling over her and capturing her mouth with mine. I wanted to melt into her, sink hip-deep and feel her on all sides of me, clutching and pumping until we were both spent. But first, a gentleman always returned favors.

I trailed my mouth across Sarah's body, shoving aside clothing, pulling down the black leggings she'd worn that day in a single feral swoop. Her pussy greeted me in a soft curl of hair, the smell of her making my mouth water. I ducked down, situating Sarah's legs over my shoulders, stretching my arms up to find her mouth-watering tits.

My hands traced the hard, twin peaks of her nipples, teasing and twisting until she was humping the air just an inch from my face.

"Harder, Chris, please." What the lady wants...

Sarah cried out, hands gripping mine through the thin t-shirt I'd slid under, the crumple of her bra against my wrists worth the light discomfort as I pinched and rolled the pert buds between my fingers.

One more thrust from her, and I covered her pussy with my mouth, lapping slowly at first until I could follow her body's rhythm, picking up pace and intensity as she twisted and moaned beneath me. I hummed against her clit, earning a faceful of juicy cunt as she practically rocketed off the mattress. Sucking on the sensitive hood, I hooked two fingers inside of her, grazing against the sweet spot that had her arching again and again.

Next door or somewhere equally far away, someone's phone was ringing.

"Chris." My name had never sounded sweeter. I continued working her higher and higher, feeling her tighten around my fingers, her hands tangling in my hair and pulling.

Man, that phone was loud.

"Chris." Her voice was urgent, her touch scorching. I added a third finger, feeling her clamp around my hand immediately. She was close. I glanced up at her, relishing the hazy, half-lidded look she gave me, the flush across her face and chest, lips plump from kissing.

I crooked all three fingers inside of her, watching her come undone as her pussy clenched and unclenched around my hand. God, I needed that to be my cock.

Lost in her orgasm, no other sounds but her screams of pleasure, I was shocked to hear her final gasp be a warning.

"Chris, your phone."

The phone that had been ringing this entire time was *mine.*

Realization slammed into me.

Swiping a hand over my mouth and chin, I pressed a quick kiss to Sarah's forehead. "I promise I'm usually better at aftercare." I hated leaving her, hated walking away from the glorious mess we'd made of each other.

But duty called—literally.

I didn't even have a chance to say hello as I tapped the answer button on my phone. "Motherfucker. I should fillet you and sell you in frozen slabs at Costco." Steve was mad.

"I'm logging in now, sorry. I got caught up in…"

Silence on Steve's end as I flipped open my laptop and frantically clicked through my email for the zoom link.

"Oh shit, sorry, did you actually want an answer to what I was doing?"

The laptop camera clicked on, and I realized I was sitting in a dark living room. Before I could reach for a window shade or lamp, blinding white light smacked me in the face. Sarah peeked out from behind her phone, wiggling her fingers at me.

She wasn't wearing anything but the thin t-shirt I'd shoved up in my haste to lavish attention on her tits.

"Joining us from an apparently gloomy San Francisco tonight is Chris Oldfelds!" The late-night host oozed charm. Applause rang out from his captive audience.

Staring at Sarah's shadowed form, knowing her bare pussy was on full display just on the other side of my laptop camera, my mouth went dry, my jaw fell slack. It was all I could do to smile back and wave.

I caught Sarah's hand gesturing in the corner of my eye—she was making the "keep going" signal, hand rolling through the air.

"Hi Jerry," I smiled wide, slipping back into my familiar movie star role. "You know how it is with Karl out here." That got a few knowing laughs and a whistle.

The rest of the interview was a blur, my dick hard again in my pants, the smell of Sarah's sex still all over me.

And in the back of my mind, a whisper getting stronger and stronger with each passing moment.

This could be my life.

SARAH

We were finally back in the theatre, immediately swallowed by the chaos of getting ready for opening night—a mere two weeks away. We wouldn't get our usual preview performances because of the rehearsal time we'd lost. We'd use what time we had to get things right and then...*open*.

The set crew had arrived the night before to install the larger pieces, hammering away at lightning speed. Costumes hung from every free edge in the building with careful handwritten notes tacked on each in Marisol's spider-like script. Angie was running gunpowder burst after gunpowder burst in the back shop making sure everything was perfect. The props master threatened to cut off fingers if anyone touched his table again.

I was in the wings, watching Chris and Nicole finish a scene, a calm, tense moment in the show that felt like the eye of the storm all around us. I found it hard to focus on their pace, losing track of the scene on the page and frantically gesturing to crew for their cues. I wasn't sure what was wrong, whether it was the jarring return to our home turf, the threat of judgement hanging over me as Chris and I entered hand-in-hand or something heavier, scarier, dancing just out of sight.

Oh.

My audition was tomorrow.

I wasn't ready. I wasn't sure I ever would be. Ever since that first practice with Chris, I'd kept it together, getting steadily closer to tolerating that sense of exposure—that feeling of eyes on me as I opened my heart to the world. And Chris was dedicated to helping me, using every free moment he had between rehearsals, press interviews, and his agent's insistent calls. He always made time to listen to me. Sometimes he offered light feedback—change my stance on one line, let the emotion come through on another—but mostly he just stared at me as if I were made of stardust.

We'd moved back to our apartments—a jarring homecoming after three weeks at the Ritz—but very little had changed about the new routine we were building. We spent every night at one apartment or the other, sleeping with Sgt. Pepper curled between us.

I'd meant what I said last week when I told Chris it felt wrong not to hear his snores in the dark. And I'd been nervous about sharing a bed together before we fell on each other like horny animals. Turns out it was as natural as if we'd been sharing a room for a decade.

But despite all the ways we grew closer, all the ways we shared the mounting tension of opening night looming and my audition on the next horizon, it seemed the *only* thing we wouldn't share with each other was what happened "after."

After the show, after my audition, after closing night.

It was as if the future was a dark, unknowable thing that hovered over us, taking all our extra energy to keep suspended.

"Can you help me, Sarah?" I snapped back to the present. Tyler, Leon's former understudy and now replacement held up his unbuttoned cuffs. "Marisol is busy with nine thousand other things. I don't want to bother her."

I nodded, setting down my notebook and quickly doing up the cumbersome tiny buttons. "She doesn't want a quick change in this, does she?"

Tyler shook his head. "Thank god, no."

"Are you getting excited?" I asked.

He smiled wide, a bright white flash in the dark. "Yes, I'm *so* excited," he said.

Tyler was young, eager, talented. His inner brilliance lit up rehearsals—I couldn't wait to see him opening night. Not to mention the relief at no longer having to deal with Leon.

"And are you?"

I looked at him, questioning.

"For your audition?" He leaned in and whispered conspiratorially.

By now it was no secret I had an audition with Alan and that, if it went well, I'd be stepping out of the wings and onto the stage. I'd been met with mixed reactions, ranging from jealousy to confusion to outright screaming joy.

"I'm more nervous than anything," I said.

"Just sing like you do at karaoke," he said. "You'll knock it out of the park without even trying."

"I don't think I can ask Alan not to look at me during a stage audition," I said, smiling as I thought of Chris saying exactly that just a few days prior.

Tyler shrugged. "You could always ask," he said, flashing me that bright smile again. "You never know."

I thought about tomorrow as Tyler walked away with a wave. Although I felt comforted by Angie and Chris requesting to sit in for moral support, I was terrified of coming apart again. Chris was supportive and caring, Angie already knew my whole story, but Alan? Who knew what his reaction would be if I came undone. I doubted it would be handing me a part.

At least I wouldn't be alone.

Vomit burned hot in my throat, and I pushed back against it, shoving aside thoughts of Alan watching my every move, notepad open on his lap.

Angie had suggested I look at Chris. "You did it at karaoke and you guys almost kissed in front of everyone. Maybe that's the trick—you just need a Chris to look at to kill your stage fright."

I'd chucked an ice cube at her in response, plucking it from my drink in the dimly lit pizza place where the three of us were sharing lunch.

She wasn't wrong. I *had* been practicing in front of Chris, singing almost directly to him every time.

There was really only one way to find out.

The next morning was foggy and ominous, a rumbling rare thunder sounding across the roof of our building. For the first time maybe ever, I was up before Chris, my nerves frazzled to bare livewires after tossing and turning all night. I rolled over and grabbed my sheet music, staring at the notes and singing the piece in my head.

"There's such a thing as being over prepared." Chris murmured next to me.

"We all have our own methods," I snipped back, not caring that stress and sleep deprivation were making me grumpy.

Chris reached an arm around, hauling me into him. I squeaked and held my sheet music up and away from the rumpled blankets.

It didn't matter how many nights we spent together. I couldn't get over the smell of him. I was more obsessed than I was at the start—it was comforting, like coming home after a long day, or walking into your childhood home after being gone for months and feeling your heart swell. I wanted to distill him into a candle. I'd make billions.

"Are you getting up?" He asked, breath warm on my neck.

"Are you?" I asked, turning to kiss the corner of his mouth.

"No, I have pressing business in this bed," he said, kissing me back.

I set the music down and gave in to him, welcoming his enveloping warmth on all sides as he rose above me. Chris settled between my legs, pressing his morning erection into my thigh as he ran his hands over my body, caressing all of me.

This was the part I knew—the part that came before sex, the part I seemed to handle just fine without the bugs returning and my anxiety taking over.

And there was always blowing him in the entryway which my mental health apparently had no issue with.

I'm a little bit of a freak—who knew?

But I was home now, in my own bed, in my own apartment. That was my crooked sunshine slanting through a broken blind, my familiar building noise as my neighbors rose, cooked, left for work, turned on their TVs.

My body was my own this morning, each of Chris' careful, gentle touches lighting up my nerves, flooding my brain, heart, soul with giddy electricity. There were no bugs, no shudders, no fears.

Chris was mine—devoted, reverent, enamored in his every movement.

And this was my moment, I decided, my day for scary things that held so much promise. I was safe. I was in control. And no one was going to shame me for seizing good things—not now. Not anymore.

I sat up, nudging Chris back with my shoulder until we were eye-to-eye.

"Do you have a condom?" I hated how business-like the request sounded in these early morning moments.

Chris searched my face, apparently not satisfied by what he found there.

"Are you sure? Today's huge for you. I don't want to—"

"I want this." I said, wrapping my arms around his neck and kissing him again. "And I need something good to think about. For later."

He kissed me back before rolling off the bed like an action hero. He was in just his boxers, beard a scruffy shadow over his sharp jawline. He made finger guns in the direction of his apartment.

"Condoms are at my place. I'll be back in a flash." He gave me a cheesy smile, threw an overexaggerated wink, and then pretended to *fly* out of the room. I laid back in bed, laughing at the sound of his bare feet thudding across the hall, his door opening and closing, more thudding from *his* apartment, and then the same door opening and closing again. When he reappeared in my bedroom doorway, he was out of breath and flushed, a roll of condoms dangling from one hand. I couldn't ignore the circus tent in his boxers.

And finally, I didn't have to.

Chris met me at the edge of the bed, our mouths crashing together like hot water over the edge of a tub. I could sink into this kiss, could let it take away my troubles, aches, and pains. I could simmer here.

But it was time to turn the heat up.

We'd been simmering. I wanted to *boil*.

I pulled Chris on top of me, reveling in the cage of his arms around my head, in the needy way he pressed against me, the thin fabric of our underwear leaving little to the imagination. Teasing fingers played along the edge of his boxers until he broke our kiss to plead.

"Sarah," he gasped, my name sweet and sacred in his mouth.

"Tell me." I pushed down his boxers, stroking him once before letting them snap back up. "Tell me what you want."

"Look at me." His voice had that rare edge that shot straight through me. I met his gaze, a little intimidated by the dark heat staring back at me. "Touch me, Sarah. Like you mean it."

This time, I shoved the boxers down all the way, gripping his shaft in one hand, caressing his balls with the other. I worked him in a steady rhythm, building up speed and grip until he sucked air through his teeth, hands grabbing my wrists and yanking them above my hand.

"You have to mean it a little less or I won't make it."

"Don't give orders you don't want executed." I grinned, pleased with myself. This man made more money than I'd ever be able to fathom, had the entertainment world in his well-manicured palm, and I'd undone him in just a few moments. *I did that.*

A muscle in his jaw twitched and something flashed in his eyes. Silently, he guided my hands up to the edge of my headboard, curling my fingers overhand so that they gripped the particle board.

"Don't let go."

Before I could process what was happening, he fell on my pussy like a starved man, sucking and lapping every inch of me until I was shaking with need. My cunt clenched around emptiness as my hands slipped from the headboard, slick with sweat.

Chris stopped immediately, pausing just long enough to place my hands back where he wanted them. He breathed a kiss on my forehead, brushed stray curls from my face.

"Beautiful," he murmured, eyes roaming over me. In another universe, Old Sarah was nervous and shy in this moment. But in the present, I couldn't think about anything but his pink, straining cock jutting out from his hips. Every part of me was vibrating with desire, my molecules reaching a frequency most often used for space travel.

"Still okay?" Chris asked, carefully guiding me to a sitting position and stripping off my nightgown. My nipples were already so sensitive that the fabric gliding over them had me gasping and squirming.

"I might die," I managed, running hungry hands over his shoulders, arms, abs, tracing down to his cock and back.

"Not before I'm done with you." He kissed me again, pulling me up to press my tits to his chest, our skin to skin, his cock against my cunt. I writhed against him, returning the kiss, desperate to touch every part of him I could all at once. Why didn't I have more hands?

With a shift of his hips, Chris' cock nudged at my entrance. The touch of him so close but so far was maddening. Before I could complain, he took my chin in one hand, tilting my face to meet his gaze.

"Tell me to stop if you need it." He said, eyes holding mine.

"Don't you dare stop." Our bodies met each other until Chris was seated to his hips, the stretch of him filling me perfectly.

"God, Sarah, you feel so good." He thrust in and out, slowly, carefully, getting the feeling for this new connection. Then, he adjusted, lifting my hips, pulling his knees closer, and withdrawing almost completely before slamming home. The angle and the friction was delicious, winding me tighter and tighter as he fucked me again and again, picking up speed.

There was no other sound but our labored breathing, the soft slap of his balls against me, the gentle hum of the city outside. The morning light slanted over us, basking our skin in a warm glow, and I wondered, briefly, if this was what it felt like to be the main character—for life to be a story with a happy ending, told over and over again for the simple joy of relishing the luck that brought us together.

Chris straightened, bringing me with him in a sitting position. His hands pressed flat against my back, keeping us close as he thrust up into me. The new angle sparked stars in my vision, and I could barely do more than cling to him as my orgasm crashed over me. Chris was close behind, thrusting through my clenching pussy, coming with a satisfied groan, teeth grazing my shoulder to muffle his cries.

Slowly, carefully, I came back to myself—sated, relaxed, happy. Chris laid us both back down, pulling the blanket over our heads to block out the sun.

No bugs. No fear. No panic.

Just us.

It was perfect.

"We're going for breakfast," Chris announced as he stepped out the shower smelling like crisp soap and man.

"We have eggs here," I said, not looking up from my sheet music.

"No ma'am," he said, wagging a finger at me. "We are not doing any extra work on audition day. We will pay some fine establishment to pour the coffee *for* us if it means you can focus."

I broke my staring contest with the measure I was reading and glanced up at him.

"*You* could make breakfast," I said.

He gasped and feigned shock, placing a hand across his chest. I smiled, remembering the first time I saw him do that in the hall those weeks ago.

"I am Chris Oldfelds. I don't make eggs. I have *people* for that," he said.

"Chris," I sighed. "I really don't think I'm gonna have much of an appetite today anyway. Why don't you go without me?"

"You have to eat, or you'll pass out before you even get on the stage."

"I'll probably do that anyway. And if I don't eat beforehand, then there won't be anything embarrassing to throw up."

Chris came around the counter where I was perched and wrapped himself around my legs. He threw his head back and cried to the ceiling.

"Please, sir, I want breakfast," he said. "Food, glorious food!"

I laughed and wiggled my legs. He clamped down on them harder, leaving a love bit on my thigh, which only made me squeal louder.

A knock came at the door.

Chris stood and answered it, throwing the door wide with a charming announcement of, "Aguilar residence, where we starve our boyfriends, how can I help you?"

Gerald glowered in the hall, cane brandished and at the ready.

"If you don't both leave already, I'll make *you* into breakfast."

"Don't threaten me with a good time," Chris waggled his eyebrows at Gerald suggestively as I collapsed into laughter, sliding off the counter.

I didn't hear what else was said, I was laughing too hard, but shortly the door was closed, and Chris was bringing me my jacket.

"Come on, I'm making a demand. Let's go."

I caved, slipping my arms into the sherpa lined sleeves of my favorite denim jacket and following Chris out the door.

He stopped me in the hall and gently tugged the sheet music from my hands.

"We both know you have this memorized," he said, reaching behind me to put it on the console table by the door. "Let the poor thing rest a moment before you abuse it further."

A shot of panic ran up my spine as he closed the door behind us, but he was right. I really did need a break.

We sprinted through the drizzle together, slipping through the foggy door of an old-school diner nearby. The blinking neon sign in the window promised "a cuppa joe," and I could tell from the peeling yellow wallpaper that I was about to fall in love with a side of bacon.

Breakfast was crisp hashbrowns, fried eggs swimming in butter, and the promised perfect, alluring bacon. We split a side of gravy when the waitress explaining it came in a soup bowl, and I braced myself for the coming day with a cup of "joe" that I could practically chew.

"I don't ever want to leave this place." Chris leaned back in the booth, patting his full stomach and stretching with a satisfied groan.

"I look forward to visiting you in your new diner," I teased him, sipping the last of my coffee.

"I meant San Francisco." He relaxed from his stretch, leaning across the table and taking one of my hands.

I let him, enjoying the warmth of his touch, but I didn't respond. What was I supposed to say? "No, stay, abandon your Hollywood career to be my boyfriend!" The check came, Chris paid, and we left in silence, sprinting back through the rain again toward the theatre.

And still, his unspoken question hung between us.

Chris stopped me before we could step into the hush of the dark theatre, rain spattering his oversized sunglasses and misting over my curls.

"Sarah—"

"Can we not?" I sighed. "I'll have whatever stressful talk you want after I'm done auditioning."

"You mean it?" He was serious, holding stone still but for his ever-dancing fingers, fidgeting at his sides.

"Yeah," I said, more than a little surprised and also largely annoyed. "If you want to talk after my audition, if you *really* feel that's the right moment for *that* conversation, then we can have it."

Chris nodded, offering his hand. I shook it.

I cursed under my breath as I stepped inside.

"Yeah," he said. "Me, too."

Chris

I was moving to San Francisco.

I'd already found a renter for my apartment in LA, had already told my agent during one of our numerous calls over the last six weeks, had already pictured LA in the rearview window of my heart.

The last week had sealed it for me. Mornings spent between the apartment I grew up in and Sarah's place, listening to her practice, running lines together, Sgt. Pepper in the middle of it all. Working hours spent with people I really enjoyed and feeling pushed to work harder than I had in years.

I wasn't leaving. Not yet.

The only problem was I hadn't told Sarah yet.

We had been dancing around the topic of the future for weeks, and she seemed particularly set on not discussing it—until it would be too late, I felt. But I was so wrapped up in her every move that I didn't care. We could keep dancing the way we were until the band gave up and the orchestra broke their chairs.

But the longer things went, the more in love I fell, the more it agitated me that she wouldn't talk to me about things. I wanted to tell her how I felt, wanted to tell her that this was not a show romance for me. I wanted to tell her how real this was and how much of a perfect chance we'd be blowing by not seeing it through—whatever that meant.

Today was the day. We'd shook on it.

And I was terrified.

It wasn't perfect and it wasn't fair. But it was done, and my stupid fear wouldn't let me back down or let it go.

The theatre was humming when we walked in, James and Greg at their usual station by the side doors.

Sarah stalked off for the wings, not so much as looking at me as we parted ways for the day.

"Whatever fight you're having," Angie said, appearing silently at my shoulder. I swear, the woman *was* the theatre ghost. "You need to *wait* until after her audition to finish it. She can't cry through 'Back to Before' and still hit her money notes."

"It'd be a brave choice, at least," I said, mimicking Alan's favorite soft criticism of actors doing something unhinged with a popular show.

"She's making enough brave choices this week," Angie said, fixing me with a knowing stare. "Let's not exhaust the hero just yet."

"Yes ma'am," I said, throwing her a salute. I headed for where the other actors were chatting in a small group by the stage.

"Everything good?" Nicole asked, giving me a side hug as I walked up.

My heart stilled, and I stared as her smile faltered. She nodded in the direction of Sarah and Angie whispering to each other behind their notebooks.

"Oh," I let loose a telling sigh and hoped no one noticed. "Just some pre-show jitters." I tried to play it off but Nicole arched an eyebrow at me, giving me a once over.

"You can tell me later, whatever that's about," she said. "Can we run the kitchen scene again, just the middle part? I'm still swapping those two lines."

I nodded and we launched into the scene. Our characters were fighting about the placement of apples on the counter as a cover for the conversation they *really* needed to have—whether or not my character was having an affair.

When we finished, Nicole satisfied with the order of her lines, I headed off to find Marisol in costuming. After that it was warmups, a few run-throughs of scenes giving us a hard time, lunch, and then, suddenly rising like a sea monster in a storm, Sarah's audition.

It would just be me and Angie in the room with Alan, everyone else going about their duties for the full-dress run-through that night. Thankfully, it seemed like everyone was so focused on getting caught up after weeks away from the theatre that there weren't too many nosy questions about where the three of us were going.

When Alan opened the door to the practice room, Sarah was there already. She'd recruited the pianist from the pit orchestra as her accompaniment.

Alan sat front and center, while Angie and I squeezed onto a spare piano bench in the very corner of the room. It was cozy with 5 adults in the room, but not uncomfortable.

I hadn't seen Sarah since our tense morning. But she looked steady and confident. My chest tightened and I clasped my sweating hands in my lap to keep from fidgeting. She'd worked tirelessly to prepare for this moment and now here we were. My stomach had butterflies *for* her.

Sarah's face split into a prizewinning smile as she greeted us, introducing herself before stepping forward dutifully and handing Alan her headshot with her resume printed on the back.

"Thank you, Sarah," he said, pushing his glasses to the edge of his nose. "What are you going to perform for us today?"

"Back to Before," she said, stepping back to her mark and nodding to the pianist.

The bars she'd chosen began, Sarah looked to me, and as we locked eyes, she began to sing.

She'd been practicing for weeks, and I'd been lucky enough to be in the room as a fly on the wall until she took Angie's off-the-wall advice. Then she started singing directly to me. She was terrified of anyone seeing her too clearly, she'd said. She felt like she was always hiding until she sang, and even then, I could see her holding back.

The hope was that when it came down to it, she'd stop hiding.

And here she was, fully present, completely visible, and owning it.

Sarah's full self came through in the song. It was like watching a tidal wave slam across the tiny room. Angie sat straight up, holding her shaking hands over her mouth. Alan pushed his glasses up to the top of his head, jaw dropped. And I couldn't move a muscle. I was entirely transfixed by the woman Sarah was shifting into in front of my eyes.

My heart ached for her, this abandoned, beautiful woman, left to fend for herself in a world made foreign to her. I wanted to whisk her off the stage and show her love as badly as I wanted to never move from my seat.

When the pianist lifted his hands from the piano, we all sat in stunned silence.

"Where the *hell* have you been, girl?" the pianist asked, breaking the silence. We erupted into applause and relieved laughter.

Alan stepped back into his director roll before he'd wiped the tears from his eyes.

"Your resume doesn't have any acting experience on it," he said. "Which, after your audition I don't expect to be an issue, but tell me why you'd be willing to make the switch from backstage?"

"Singing sets me free." Sarah glanced at her feet, then pulled her gaze back up, locking eyes with Alan. "And I love this theatre more than anywhere else in the city. It'd be a dream to start my new journey here."

Alan nodded, mouth curving into a soft smile.

"We'd be honored to see you launch," he said. He stood and offered his hand to Sarah who shook it. "Welcome to the company Miss Aguilar. I don't know what part you'll sing yet, but you *will* sing."

Sarah burst into tears as he pulled her into happy embrace.

"Now, I believe your loved ones would like to congratulate you," he said, sketching a tiny bow and nodding to the pianist. The two left, squeezing by us as we erupted into joyful screaming.

Angie and Sarah hugged, shrieking at the top of their lungs, twirling in a circle. "I fucking *told you*," Angie whispered into Sarah's hair before pulling away. "I fucking *told* you!"

"You were right." Sarah rolled her eyes, but the grin stayed.

"Thank you!" Angie booped her nose before nodding toward the door. "And with that, I have so much work to do. I gotta go." She blew me a kiss as she sashayed to the door in a whirl of gleaming black hair. "Don't fuck in here, I'll *know*."

Sarah blew her a kiss as Angie stepped out of the room, leaving the two of us alone.

"So," she said, letting her voice trail off into the sudden silence of the room.

"You were amazing," I said, closing the small distance between us to crush her against my chest. "Just so, *so* amazing."

"I'm have a part," she whispered.

"Probably a big one," I said.

"No," she shook her head against me and her curls sent up a waft of her shampoo.

"I've never seen Alan cry during an audition," I said. "You're getting a good part."

"I can't even believe it," she said, looking up at me, brown eyes glittering with tears.

"Start believing," I said. "Cause it's happening."

She sighed happily against me, leaning her chin on my shoulder. Then she gave me a nudge and stepped an arm's length away, twining her fingers with mine.

"You wanted to talk now, didn't you?"

"If now's okay?" My stomach flip-flopped, flinging my heart into my throat. For the first time in decades, I was truly nervous.

Sarah glanced at the door, then back to me, this time her posture more resolute. She nodded.

"I'm moving here," I blurted out, watching her eyes grow so big they nearly ate her forehead.

"Excuse me?"

"I'm moving to San Francisco," I said. "I don't want to be in LA anymore. I don't care what the consequences are to my career. This feels right."

"This," she gestured between us. "Or this," she continued, jabbing a finger at the floor.

"Both," I said. If I scared her off now, I'd never forgive myself, but I couldn't hold it in anymore. "I'll regret it for the rest of my life if I don't give us a chance. I want to see where we go together."

Fresh tears slid down her cheeks, and she wrestled her fingers from mine to cover her face.

"Are these good tears or bad tears?"

Silence.

I gave it a few more moments before Sarah angrily swiped her hands across her cheeks, leveling an accusatory finger at me.

"You made me wait *all day* for the best news of my *life?*" She jabbed the finger into my chest. "You're a *sick* man."

I leaned down and kissed her, rubbing my thumbs across her cheeks to wipe away the tears.

"Wouldn't the audition be the best news of your life?" I asked, kissing her forehead.

"It should've been," she sobbed. "You're such a show-stealer."

"Sarah," I whispered into her hair. "I need to hear that you're okay with this."

"Of course I'm okay with it," she said, sniffling. "I'm not ready for us to end yet."

"Me neither," I said, a smile cracking my face open.

"Hey, you two," Angie swung the practice room door open. "There's an early dinner from catering. We have to start soon."

We followed Angie out of the room and back up to where everyone else was, fingers tightly woven together with no intention of separating.

SARAH

I felt like I was floating. My life had changed for the better in so many ways, in just an hour. I was going to sing in the cast. I was going to step onto the stage for the first time ever. Chris was staying in San Francisco—*moving* to San Francisco.

If my heart got any lighter, I was going to drift up to the rafters and never come down.

Final-dress was planned for tonight, so cast and crew alike were gathered, munching on catered sandwiches, chatting quietly together before silence would descend across the building as the lights lowered. Snatches of conversation bounced around the stage, and I let myself melt into the background, energized to be in the same room with people I loved being, in the theatre where I planted my heart only for it to grow in unexpected ways.

It was perfect.

"I've never seen anyone accept bad news with such elation," Rebecca sauntered over to me and Chris. "I'm assuming the audition went well. When can we expect you to join us, Sarah?"

I shrugged, wary of her congratulations given our last conversation.

"I'll hear from Alan after the opening," I said, hoping the answer was enough to placate her fangs.

"Good for you," she demurred, pursing her lips and floating away. I let out a quiet exhale.

"Don't let her get to you," Chris said. "It's not about you, remember?"

I nodded, looking around at the gathered cast. My rosy warmth was quickly dimming. "Do you think anyone else feels the way she does?"

"What do you mean?"

"I don't know, like I'm using you for my own gain?"

"Anyone who matters doesn't think that," he said. "Besides, how do they know I'm not using *you*?"

I arched an eyebrow at him, and he held his hands out in innocence. "What? Do you blame me for trying to ride the coattails of the next Patti Lupone?"

Marisol rescued me from such lavish praise, waving for Chris to join her. But not before I pinched his side as I shoved him toward the costumer.

"You're needed," I said.

I watched him go with Marisol, sticking my tongue out at him as he blew a silent kiss across the stage.

"You two are gross," Angie said from over my shoulder.

"I'm going to put a bell on you," I said, jumping out of my skin.

"Many greater than you have tried and failed," she said, making her hand into claws and hissing at me.

"How're the ballistics today?" I asked, letting her swipe a few chips from the bag in my hands.

"Extra explodey," she said, grinning like an animal and chomping down on the chip.

"I can't wait to see them tonight," I said.

"How do you think this is all gonna go," she said waving her hands at the stage and those assembled.

I shrugged. "We've been in worse spots before opening," I said. "We've always found a way out."

"We've been in worse spots than not being allowed into the theatre for a month before opening?"

I sighed. "Please don't ask me for an example."

"Continuing to excel at lying to ourselves, I see." She threw me a wink as Alan stood, dusting chip crumbs from his pants.

"Alright everyone, take an extra fifteen minutes to stretch, go for a walk, get whatever provisions you need next. And then we're going to start. We won't be stopping."

"That's a big 'if,'" Angie muttered, crossing her arms. I shushed her, listening to the rest of Alan's instructions.

"I know we're all stressed about executing with perfection," he said. "And while I admire that in you as my fellow artists, let's remember people come to live theatre to be entertained. A little chaos adds to the spice of the show."

He clapped his hands and everyone scattered, sprinting for a snack run or beginning complex yoga movements where they stood. Chris still hadn't come back from the costume department yet, so I followed Angie to the shop to help her finish what she needed for the gunshot sounds.

She had several small containers packed tightly and duct taped with a military-like precision. We wanted to give the audience the sensory experience of a gun going off—the smell of the gunpowder, the crack of the bullet without risking fatal accidents from shooting blanks. Angie rigged these small, bottle-rocket like packages that would give those sensations when triggered at the same time as the actor pretended to fire a round.

Tonight was the first time we'd be using them in tandem with the show. Chris had a show-clinching line right as he pretending to shoot and if the effect went off too early, the audience would miss it. If it went off too late, the spell would be broken.

Excitement sang through as Angie showed me where place each container. I loved this part of my job—keeping the magic going after the actors took their places, helping to weave illusion and immersion.

"You know," Angie said, when we were done, picking up our binders and double-checking if we'd missed anything. "This won't be me and you anymore once you're an actor."

It would have hurt less if she'd punched me in the stomach. My hand ghosted to my waist, as if I could soothe the ache building there.

"What're you talking about?"

"You'll be a big-shot musical actor," she said, not looking up at me. "You're not gonna come backstage and help me set and strike."

"Angie..." I didn't know what to say.

"I'm happy for you, Sarah," she said. "And I could never hold you back. But I'm gonna miss you like crazy."

For the first time, I felt the world shift under my feet as I realized that she was right. I'd stepped over the edge, tipping into an entirely new world—one where I didn't know the rules anymore. I didn't even know who I'd be in this new space.

Alan's voice rang through the wings, calling for places. The scrambling thud of feet meant everyone was in place, cutting off my whirling thoughts and pulling me back to focus.

The lights went down, the sound system played the opening theme, and various bodies whizzed by me for the stage, sending the partition curtains rustling in the dark.

The lights slowly raised as the curtain pulled back and, there, in a perfect vignette of a 1950s family, were Chris and Nicole for their opening scene.

I followed the script carefully, calling into the headset on cue and helping the crew move seamlessly through the first act. I latched onto the excitement of executing something we'd been working on for so long, feeling the shared thrill roll down my spine with tingling sparks.

A few props were missed, a few entrances were late, but overall, the first act went smoothly. The curtains closed for intermission and Alan called out from the House seats.

"Good work so far everyone, we'll use a real fifteen."

That meant we only had a true intermission length to strike and reset the stage. I stepped out of the way as the actors sprinted to change, and crew members moved back and forth with various set pieces.

"Sarah," Chris whispered nearby, and I found him, barely lit by the red backstage light we kept on so people wouldn't trip. He had changed into his costume for the opening of act two—a simple swap of a sportscoat and tie.

"How does it feel?" I asked, smoothing his tie for him. He looked like someone out of a GQ cover in a suit, and I felt a strange tremor in my knees realizing he'd done a GQ cover in a suit.

"Amazing," he said. "I can't believe I waited this long to come back to theatre. I feel so *alive!*"

He kissed me quickly, squeezing my elbows as he let me go. He was passionate, electric, and...kind of nerdy. Whatever, it worked on me.

"Break your limbs," I whispered as Alan called out the 1-minute warning, and he sprinted for the stage.

A warmth and joy spread in my chest that I didn't have a name for. But I couldn't wait to explore it further. Here. With him.

The second act was not nearly as energizing. A set piece fell, crashing to the stage and halting the run for several precious minutes while it was repaired. Chris bungled his lines for the kitchen scene, which meant Nicole tripped up and lost hers as well. And if that wasn't enough, Angie's blasts never sounded, meaning they were not only dysfunctional, but a hazard.

When the curtain finally closed on the ending, a collective groan went up from the crew.

"Alright, everyone," Alan said as the curtain opened back up, and we all filed out for notes. Not a single set of shoulders sat straight. "Remember what they say about a bad dress—we'll have a killer opening!" No one smiled back at him. He cleared his throat. "It was a little rough at the end there, but nothing we can't fix."

"We're going to be here all night," someone moaned from the back.

"Well, with that attitude," Alan snipped. "Everyone take five. You look like you need fresh air."

"Are we allowed to go outside, or will we be besieged by photographers?" Rebecca asked from where she'd flopped onto the stage couch.

"Only one way to find out," Chris snapped, pinching the bridge of his nose. I took his hand in warning.

"Take the five or I'll start notes *now,*" Alan flapped his hands at us, scattering cast and crew alike across the theatre. I heard the backstage door open, and I tugged Chris toward it, desperate to breath air that hadn't been recirculating for the last twelve hours.

Rain had come and gone while we'd been in the dark, and the air smelled of fresh, wet garbage.

"Mmmm." Chris nodded, inhaling deep. "That's the city I remember."

The prop master shared a cigarette with Marisol a few steps away from us, their foreheads pressed together, murmuring quietly. A clear evening sky stretched overhead, slanting rose gold light over Chris' glowing blonde hair, giving him an unnatural tan. I was so wrapped up in the stunning portrait in front of me, I didn't notice the concern in his eyes until he spoke.

"We're okay?"

"Why wouldn't we be?"

"I thought, maybe you'd have second thoughts, once you had more time to think about things."

I shook my head, unsure where this was all coming from. "Is that why you jumped your lines? You were worried?"

He shrugged one shoulder.

My heart clenched and I couldn't help the soft laugh that escaped into the crisp air. "That's...really cute." Chris let out a long exhale, running a hand over his face. "But please don't ruin the show because you're second-guessing yourself." I stepped closer, closing the distance between us, sliding my arms around his waist. "I'm happy you're giving us a real chance. And I could've never done what I did today without you—your support."

"That's not true."

"It *is*. I took the audition to get Angie off my back, but I had every intention of failing it...I just wanted to stop being haunted by fucking Mr. Thompson, but then you were there, wanting the best for me. And I decided I wanted the best for me, too."

I couldn't read the emotion on his face, but it was shining with something intense and earnest. I wasn't sure I was ready for it.

"Production is incredible, and I love my job, but I was living in fear. That's no way to live."

I watched Chris' face in slow motion, watched the way his gaze deepened, felt his hands grip my shoulders, tried not to duck at the wave of earnestness he was about to drop on me.

"I—"

"Time to head back in." Marisol cut him off, waving from the back door she was holding open.

"Those notes aren't gonna take themselves," Chris said, dropping his hands and gesturing for me to lead. Disappointment fluttered behind me like a shadow I'd never noticed before.

"What were you going to say?"

"Sarah, Chris, come on." Angie poked her head out behind Marisol.

"One second," I snapped.

Chris looked from Angie to Marisol then back to me, uncertainty sparking through his fidgeting limbs. Finally, after a last long breath, he shook his head.

"Now's not the time." He planted a kiss on my forehead before striding past me, back to the dark.

I tried to shake off an impending sulk, unsure of what Chris had started to say, but my gut was telling me it was important. Time itself had slowed for the reveal, so why was he backing off now?

I couldn't stew for long. When we reached the stage, Alan was in a heated discussion with his back to us. It wasn't until Chris cleared his throat, that the director shifted his body enough for us to see the recipient of his anger.

Leon was back.

Chris

I wanted to leap off the stage, punch Leon in his smug face, and maybe not stop until it wasn't so smug. But Sarah wrapped herself around my arm, holding tight. I'd have to settle for yelling.

"Gutsy move, coming back here."

He didn't even flinch.

"Chris, I'll handle this." Alan's voice was steely.

Excited whispers erupted around the room and small groups formed across the stage, like a poorly made roux, clumping in the pan.

"Twenty bucks to punch his teeth in," Marisol whispered, wandering over to me and Sarah. "You're the only one with a lawyer good enough to get away with it."

I shook my head. "I'm already under fire for the rumors Leon started," I said. "It would only hurt the production for me to act out."

"Oh, you haggling?" Marisol arched her eyebrows at me. Over her shoulder I could see Alan continuing to argue with Leon. "I only have the twenty, Mr. Hollywood."

"Marisol," Sarah hissed through her teeth.

But the costumer wasn't the only one invested in my involvement. Several pairs of eyes glanced at me from whispered conversations, darting to Leon and back.

I reluctantly let go of Sarah's hand and went to Alan, interrupting the tense conversation.

"What do you want?" Leon sneered.

"I want to see if there's anything I can do to resolve this problem," I said through gritted teeth.

"That's not necessary, Chris," Alan said, placing a hand on my shoulder.

"We have a second act to fix," I said. "Before tomorrow. We don't need whatever trouble this yahoo wants to bring in here. How did you get in, anyway?"

"This was my home before it was yours," Leon said, jaw clenched. "I have my ways of getting around undetected."

"You sound like a supervillain," I said. "Come on, Leon, what do you *want?*"

"Actually," he looked thoughtful before continuing. "There is something you can do to solve my problem."

"Anything that gets you out the door."

"A million dollars."

"No."

"That will solve it," he shrugged, as nonchalantly as if he'd asked me to cat sit for him. "You took work from me—from a local actor who deserved that part. And now I'm struggling." He arched a brow. "I know it's within your means to offer a solution."

"The answer is no."

"Leon, *really.*" Alan was gripping his folio so tightly his knuckles were white.

"500, then. $500,000 and I'll leave right now and never come back."

"No."

"You *are* haggling," Marisol called out from the far side of the stage. I was suddenly aware of the abnormally silent stage. Not a single tiptoe creaked across the floor. The air hung heavy with expectation, and my skin crawled with all the eyes on me.

"$100k," I said, jutting my chin at Leon defiantly. "Paid through my lawyer. On the record."

Leon considered me for a moment, a sneer growing on his face.

"And you'll have to sign an agreement that you'll stay away from me, Sarah, and this theatre."

"Chris," Alan's voice was a low warning.

"You wanna buy me off *and* put me out of work?" Leon gasped, loud enough that everyone could definitely hear, not just Marisol's expert eavesdropping.

"Fine," I hissed. "Just that you have to stay away from me so long as I'm working here."

"Can't imagine that'll be much longer," he snarled.

"Leon!" Alan snapped.

"I want a quarter mil," he said. $250,000. This man was never going to stop until he got what he wanted.

"Don't, Chris!"

"Do it! Fuck that guy!"

"Hey, I want $100k! Do I have to be a douchebag to get it?"

"Fine," I said, trying and failing to block out everyone's growing opinions. I held out my hand. Leon took it and we shook, despite Alan's spluttering protests.

"Expect paperwork from my lawyer tomorrow."

"Pleasure doing business with you," Leon purred. He threw his arms wide as I turned to walk away from him, blood threatening to boil over.

"I hope everyone here knows that their hometown hero just paid a bribe to keep his dirty business on the down low," he called out.

"Get *out*, Leon," Nicole called. Several others joined her in a chorus of jeers and boos, waving him out.

Leon turned on his heel and left, flipping everyone off as he did so. I didn't take my eyes off his back until the House doors closed behind him.

I pulled out my phone and shot off an angry text to both James and Greg for having let that risk through on their watch.

"Chris?"

"*What*," I snapped, looking up to see Sarah flinch.

"I was going to ask if you're okay," she said, stepping back from me. "But clearly that was a mistake." She stormed off before I could apologize, leaving me on the stage surrounded by staring cast and crew.

Alan cleared his throat, breaking the shocked silence.

"Places, from the top of Act Two. We have work to do, folks. Can't allow personal business to interrupt."

"Is *that* what that was?" Angie asked as she walked by. Slowly, the stage cleared, leaving me and Nicole. Before we took our places, she reached over and squeezed my shoulder.

"I get it," she said.

"That's not as comforting as you think it is," I said, letting out a deep breath and trying to sink back into my character.

"Just don't pay off every emo weirdo that comes through the doors," she said. "You'll burn through that superhero money real fast."

I didn't have time to respond before the curtains closed, and the second act theme came from the speakers. I knew she was right. But I felt helpless, and I was honestly relieved for an end to the conversation.

I didn't know what else I was supposed to do. If money could solve the singular thorn in our collective sides—and I had the money—then what was the problem? Ignoring Leon felt too much like the mouse who kept walking past the lion.

It wasn't right or fair to let everyone else suffer because I was scared about what might happen.

Nicole and I launched into our scene, and I felt my character take over. My mind quieted as it slipped into recitation. I let the anger my body still held fuel the character choices, and by the time the scene was over, a strange calm settled in my limbs.

As if I needed another reminder of why I was in the right place for this chapter of my life. Acting on a movie set never provided this kind of relief, this specific brand of quiet balance and emotional processing. There was something about the stage and its timbre that offered me release.

If falling in love with Sarah hadn't clinched the deal for me, this would've done it. I needed to be on stage. I needed to be in San Francisco.

And there wasn't a single person in this world who was going to take that away from me.

It was past midnight by the time we left the theatre, Sarah and I stumbling into a private car that drove us the short distance back to our apartments.

"I want to sleep alone tonight," she said as we made our way up the stairs.

"What?" My stomach plummeted through the floor. It seemed like all our lovestruck elation from earlier that afternoon was entirely deflated.

"I don't like how you are right now," she said, shoving her key in her door and doing the usual complicated dance to open it. "I want some space."

That was the last thing she said to me for the night, letting her door click silently shut behind her.

I stuck my own key in the door, but for some reason, I couldn't get the latch to turn. I was about to slam my shoulder into the door when I heard a familiar voice from down the hall.

"That door giving you trouble?" It was Gerald's wife, Betty, who I'd only heard call out from the far end of their apartment. Seeing her now for the first time, snow-white curls puffing out from her rounded face, I felt a memory spark to life that had been lying dormant.

"Mrs. Normandy?" I asked, squinting at her.

"Chris?" She gasped. I watched her slowly make her way out the door before clearing the distance between the two of us down the hall.

"I barely recognize you! Has it been your handsome voice all this time?"

"I didn't know you were still here. I would've knocked on your door," I said. "Although your husband might not have appreciated it."

Mrs. Normandy rolled her eyes, laughing. "Ronny passed away a few years back," she said. "Gerald's my boyfriend. Don't mind him, he's a bit of a grump."

"I never took you for the type to shack up with a grump," I said, throwing her a wink.

She laughed, pinching my arm. "You rascal," she said. "You haven't changed. Well, aside from growing quite a bit. Who let you get this tall?"

"Men grow, Betty, leave it be!" Gerald called from back in the apartment. Mrs. Normandy rolled her eyes again, giving me a nudge.

"You go on and get some rest, it's late. Come by this weekend."

"I can't, the show—"

"You can," she said, fixing me with a stare. "Your mama wouldn't take any excuses about it if she were here, god rest her soul."

I nodded. She was right. "Yes ma'am, I'll see you this weekend."

"Oh, and Chris, that door," she said, turning around before closing her own door. "Remember you have to lift *and* pull."

I followed her instructions, the door popping open without much more effort.

When I turned around to thank her, she was already gone, the hallway silent.

I stepped into my own dark apartment, hearing the soft thump of Sgt. Pepper coming to greet me from the back bedroom.

I immediately missed Sarah, wished I could fall asleep holding her. I wasn't looking forward to a night of tossing and turning from pre-show jitters, no slumbering Sarah to soothe me.

Sgt. Pepper gave me a curious meow, sitting down with a heavy thud in the kitchen.

"Yeah," I said. "It makes sense we'd have our first fight this week. You're right. We *are* under a lot of stress."

More meowing and a few less-than-gentle scratches on my leg as I stepped into the kitchen and grabbed him a can of wet food.

"No," I said. "I still don't know if I did the right thing. There's only one way to find out, and it involves a *lot* of waiting."

Sgt. Pepper was done with our one-sided conversation, however, as he his only response to me now was hungry chomps and slurps.

"Gross," I sighed, making my way to the back bedroom. I fell down face first on top of the blankets, kicking off my shoes and wiggling under the covers. Thankfully, sleep took me before my brain could rile me up any further.

Sarah

The next morning, I woke practiced what I would say to Chris as we walked for coffee.

"I can't control how you spend your money," I said to the mirror picking up my toothbrush. "But it feels like you paid off a kidnapper before they ran off with your baby."

That didn't sound right.

"It feels like you gave in to the bad guy," I said, gesturing with my toothpaste tube. "Okay yeah that's closer. Kidnapping a baby...God, Sarah."

I brushed my teeth, thinking through the next part. I spit, rinsed, then tried again.

"You can just throw money around like that," I said. "Like, why not throw some at me?"

I groaned in frustration. "Nope, not that."

The truth was, I couldn't figure out how to explain to Chris why I was mad at him after yesterday. I knew he was only doing what he thought was right—what he thought would make life easier for everyone. Here again was another strange moment where how little we knew about one another was dragged into stark lighting.

I'd never dated anyone with so much expendable income before. It bothered me that he seemed so careless with it—even if his motivation was filled to the brim with caring. But to throw away more money than I'd ever seen in my life—as if it were *nothing*. My stomach flipped, not for the first time, just trying to wrap my head around it.

What I needed to do—and what I was absolutely avoiding—was ask Chris for his side. He probably had some reasoning that would make it all make sense, and I could let it go.

"$250,000 would solve a lot of problems for a lot of people," I said to my reflection, finally clicking off the bathroom light and going into the hall. "Seems a shame to blow it all on getting one asshole to clear off."

"Is that why you needed space last night?" Chris called from my living room. I froze in horror, forgetting briefly that I'd given him a spare key.

He was standing near my door, two cups of coffee in his hands, his coat dusted with droplets from the morning mist.

"How long have you been there?"

"For at least three of your practice takes," he said. He offered me a sad half smile.

"I don't know what to say," I said.

He shrugged and handed me a coffee. "I think you've tried to say most of what you could," he said. "It's okay."

I nodded, feeling stupid, and sipped my coffee.

"Thank you," I said, holding the cup up. "This is nice."

"Not $250,000 nice, huh?"

"That's not what this is about."

"It is a little bit," he shrugged. "It's okay if it is. We should talk openly about money. I can arrange a call with my accountant and financial advisor if you'd like to better understand things."

"No, no," I waved a hand through the air. "That's your business it doesn't involve me."

"It does if it makes you this uncomfortable," he said.

"I just." I sighed. "It feels weird. It feels weird that you gave in to Leon. That you could spend that kind of money without thinking."

"It makes life easier for a lot of people," he said. "It'll mean no more interruptions to the show, no more energy sucked from Alan, and no more stress for Marisol."

"Marisol can handle herself," I said, thinking of the firm set of her jaw every time Leon came into the department sniffing around.

"And it's money that I have," he said. "I don't care about buying nice things. Mom's medical bills are paid off. I rent my apartment. There's not a lot hanging over my head for me to worry about."

"You don't think he'll come back and try to get more out of you?"

"That's why he has to agree to a contract. It's binding by law that in no uncertain terms, he gets his money but then has to leave me alone."

"Until he figures out a different kind of blackmail," I said, not buying into Chris' optimism about the whole situation.

He sighed. "I may have acted a little hasty," he said. "But I was angry and scared. And you and I were...we made this...I was going to..." He gestured uselessly with his free hand, face burning bright red. "I didn't want Leon coming in and mucking everything up with his..." He wiggled his fingers and scowled. "Leon-ness."

I laughed, feeling a little lighter.

"Well, when you put it that way." I rolled my eyes. But against my will, Chris' charm was working on me. "I shouldn't judge how you spend your money anyway. You're right. It solves a problem."

"And that's what it's there for."

"It's…a lot."

"Worse than the movie star paparazzi stuff?"

"Way worse."

"We'll have a lot of adjustments, you and me. I'm willing to swing the dial if you are."

What wasn't he willing to do for me? For the "us" that was beginning in all the most beautiful parts of my life?

I sighed, sipping my coffee.

"I am. But please no more split-second quarter-mill purchases without warning."

"Agreed." Chris held his arms out. "Kiss me and makeup?"

"Ooo, my favorite game," I said, practically skipping into his arms and planting one on him.

Although neither of us had to be to work until much later that afternoon, we were used to our morning coffee walks. The city was quiet beneath the fog, muffling our voices as we tried to pump one another up for the big night.

Turning a corner, hand-in-hand, it was nice to feel something resembling normal. We strolled through parklets, gawked at lush patio gardens, filled each other in on the things we'd missed in all the chaos the last few days.

Chris told me about Betty and how he was expected to visit over the weekend.

"Please go with me," he said. "I'm sure Mrs. Normandy will tell you embarrassing stories about me."

"You sure you don't want time together?" I asked. "I don't want to intrude."

"Honestly, you'd be doing me a favor," he said, looking down at the sidewalk as we neared our favorite deli. "I don't know if I can talk about my mom with her alone."

I squeezed his hand, pulling him down to kiss me at the stoplight.

"Whatever you need, I'll do it," I said. And I meant it.

"Perfect execution in and out of the theatre," he said. "How'd I get so lucky?"

"Not too many actors go rooting around in the wings," I said. "Your adventurous spirit probably had something to do with it."

"All the more for me then," he said, looping an arm around my shoulders and pulling me into his side as we crossed the street.

Inside, we cut through shelves of snacks and ready-made items, only stopping once we reached the tiny, crammed deli counter in the back. The menu was faded yellow, the prices crossed out, rewritten, then crossed out again. Handwritten signs on notebook paper curled around the edges, advertising specials and new menu items.

It wasn't fancy, but no one in the city made a sandwich like Lucy.

As if on cue, the wire-haired Italian woman surfaced from the back room, her apron snug around her round form, slipping her gnarled knuckles into clear plastic gloves.

"What's for today?" she asked. I went with a meatball sub, and Chris got turkey stacked with so many additions I wasn't sure he'd be able to bite into it. Lucy waved at us to sit.

"Are you worried about tonight at all?" I asked as we settled into rickety chairs. His sneakers tapped against the scuffed linoleum.

"I feel like I'm three seconds away from throwing up every minute," he said.

"Really? But haven't you done this a thousand times?"

"Well, you're watching, for one," he said. "You make me nervous." The way he blushed when he said it nearly sent my head spinning off my neck. I wanted to kiss every freckle across the heating skin on his face.

"I'd offer to close my eyes, but I will be working," I said, settling for taking his hand across the table.

Lucy called out from behind the register, and Chris stood, paying for the food before returning to our crooked table. I thought briefly about how not so long ago, I'd been terrified of him paying for anything. I'd been so scared that everyone would think I was getting special treatment.

"Can I tell you something else?" He asked as I chomped into the delicious Dutch crunch, a hard-topped bread that made San Francisco sandwiches an *event*. And through some unknown magic, Lucy place had the *best* Dutch crunch in town.

"This will be the first show my mom isn't there for," he said, looking down at his untouched sandwich. It was stacked higher than I'd anticipated. "She made me feel brave. Whenever I couldn't remember a line or felt overwhelmed by all those people watching me, I'd find her in the crowd. Knowing she was there helped me breathe."

I reached across the table and squeezed his hand.

"I'm so sorry, Chris," I said around an embarrassingly large bite of sandwich. "I was I could offer you a good replacement, but there isn't one."

He nodded. "Thanks," he said. "I'm hoping it helps me heal, doing this show without her. I think she'd want me to, even if she can't be here."

An idea took shape in the back of my mind. Maybe a disaster, maybe a delight. I wanted to try, regardless. I had just told him I'd do anything to help. And I wanted to make him feel the way I had in that audition room—safe, seen, supported.

Although it meant introducing myself to Mrs. Normandy—alone.

"Hey," I said, wrapping my sandwich up in the extra tin foil on my plate. "I actually have some stuff I told Angie I'd help with. You should take the bus out to the botanical gardens. It'll help clear your head."

Before he could protest, I kissed his forehead and took off. I checked over my shoulder to make sure he wasn't behind me before I doubled back to our building.

Hopefully, Mrs. Normandy was already home.

CHRIS

As soon as the curtains pulled open and the lights hit us, every nerve in my body caught fire.

I could rehearse 24-hours a day, 7 days a week, and still never be fully prepared for 400 pairs of eyes staring at me under a spotlight. The soft rustle of programs flipping, legs readjusting, all those breaths inhaling and exhaling. If I focused on it too, I'd go crazy.

Thankfully, I had way too much to juggle in my head—lines, energy, breath, Sarah, Mom, tonight.

Act One launched smoothly. The energy was fresh, bouncing from us, off the ceiling, through the audience, where it converted and returned to us.

Performing for a camera would *never* compare to this. Not in a billion years.

As I exited for a costume change, I got a bunch of silent thumbs up and smiles. Sarah gave me a peck on the cheek in-between her other duties. I felt unstoppable.

And then we got to the kitchen scene.

Nicole swapped her lines like she'd been struggling with for weeks, but I'd already prepared myself for that. I had backup responses ready to make the scene make sense and to steer her back on course in case she got confused or lost her place in her memorization.

But then someone whispered in the front row, and I completely froze. I don't know what they said or if it was even a full whisper and not a muttered sneeze. But since Nicole said the wrong line, I no longer knew which line to offer next.

I stared at Nicole, who stared back at me. She offered the line again, still wrong. The silence stretched between us and out across the audience. Feet shuffled impatiently. Then Nicole said her line correctly, eyes pleading in apology. But it wasn't enough. I was still frozen.

Suddenly, my chest felt tight, the room spinning around me. Without realizing it, I scanned the crowd for Mom. But when reality kicked in—that she wouldn't be there, ever again, tears slammed hot behind my eyes.

"Darling, don't be foolish." Someone stage-whispered from the wings.

I looked around, trying to figure out why someone would choose to tease me now.

"Darling, don't be foolish," the voice whispered again.

Now it was hard to stand. My legs buckled beneath me, and if I didn't sit down soon I was going to pass out. I sat next to Nicole, who gripped my hand as if her hands were made of steel. Someone in the audience cleared their throat loudly as we sat there in silence.

"Darling, don't be foolish," the voice said, louder this time.

"I'm not being foolish," Nicole said, finally continuing the scene without me. But whatever had just happened to me, I couldn't break free from it. My breathing came in ragged gasps. The world was threatening to tilt out from under me.

I shook my head, dragging in sharp breath after sharp breath.

"We'll discuss this another time, come, let us away." Nicole improvised me to safety, helping me stand and leading me carefully into the wings. The curtain fell. Somewhere far away, I hard Alan's voice over the speaker. Something about a technical break, thank you for your patience. A wave of whispers washed against the curtain, breaking as if against a rocky shore.

Someone pressed a bottle of water into my hand as a cool cloth was pressed to the back of my neck.

"Just breath, Chris," Nicole said, bending over me. "It's okay, just take some deep breaths."

Sarah found us, sitting next to me and taking my other hand. She rubbed soothing circles on my back and slowly, piece by piece, I was able to come back to myself, wrangling my thoughts to stillness. I heaved a sigh like I'd just surfaced above the water after holding my breath, regaining my focus and feeling in my limbs.

"Good," Sarah cooed, continuing her soothing circles.

"Chris!" Alan called, shoving his way through the crowd of cast and crew. "What happened? Are you alright?"

All I could do was nod.

"Can you go back on?"

I nodded again.

"You have to say something to me, Chris, so I know you're well enough to say your lines."

"I'm sorry, Alan," I said, voice shaking. "That's never happened before, I don't know what's wrong."

"It's a panic attack," Sarah said quietly, continuing to rub circles around my back.

"Can you go back on?" Alan asked, eyes soft with concern. "We can call in Carson for the night."

"It's opening night, I have to be there," I protested, feeling my chest squeeze tight again.

"Nothing matters more than your health," Alan said. "I'll have Carson get ready in case you change your mind."

"He'll just be disappointed!" I called after Alan's retreating form, feeling embarrassed by how much I was letting my pride take over.

"You can try again tomorrow, Chris," Sarah said, squeezing my shoulder. I shook her off.

"I don't want to," I said. "I want to do it tonight. It's important to me that I do this tonight."

"Why?"

I covered my face, willing hot tears to stay in place.

"Because if I can't do it tonight, I can't do it ever again."

Sarah wrapped her arms around me, and I leaned into her, comforted by the smell of her shampoo, the warmth of her presence.

"You *can* do it every other night," she said. "You don't have anything to prove here."

"I have to prove it to myself," I said. "I have to prove to myself that I don't still need my mom to hold my hand for the first night."

Sarah sighed against me.

"We all still need our moms to hold our hands," she said. "There's no shame in that. But if that's what's throwing you off, can you visualize your mom in the crowd?"

"She's not there," I sniffled, mortification building with each tear that squeezed out.

"You don't know that for sure," Sarah said. "And what if she was? In one form or another? What would that look that? What would it feel like?"

I thought about the warmth and joy I felt before the curtain opened, how excited I was to perform with Nicole and to return backstage to Sarah. I thought about the glitter of the stage lights flashing across glasses and wristwatches in the audience. I thought about the magical way theatre could make a room full of people believe a pile of plywood and paint was another place and time.

"It would feel just like it does now," I said.

"And if all else fails, just remember to take a deep breath when you forget a line or freeze up. All your brain needs is a little oxygen."

I nodded, sitting upright and staring at Sarah. She reached over and wiped the tears off my cheeks.

"You're a miracle," I said.

She shook her head. "Just another human with anxiety," she said, smiling softly at me.

"How are we?" Alan appeared again, twisting his hands together.

"Ready," I said, standing back up.

"Are you sure? Carson—"

"I'm sure," I cut him off.

Alan nodded in silence, worry pulling at the corners of his face.

"Alright, everyone," he clapped his hands together. "Places in five!"

Nicole brought her emergency touch up kit to the wings, dusting across my face where tears had left streaks in my stage makeup.

I thanked her, she looped her arm in mine, and we strolled onto the stage as the curtain opened.

She took her seat on the sofa, and I returned to my mark, delivering my opening line for the scene. This time, Nicole didn't hesitate, and even though I could see the great yawning expanse of the audience next to us, I took a deep breath and continued the scene. I imagined in that expanse, my mom was sitting and watching, just like she'd always done every time before.

And even if she wasn't physically in the room, the warmth and support I felt from the wings was enough to remind me that she could be there in other ways. I just had to do my best and wait for her to appear.

The scene continued without further interruption, and I was relieved when the curtain closed on the act. I worried that another panic attack would creep up on me every time I took a pause to bring up the next line or as I thought through a tense moment in character. I was shaking as I exited the stage, sitting down heavily in the green room and holding my head in my hands.

"Still okay?" Nicole asked, sitting next to me and handing me a fresh bottle of water.

"I don't know," I said, shaking my head. "I think I can get through the show, but this is not the opening night I envisioned for all of us."

Nicole shrugged. "We find ways to get through it," she said. "Even better if you can channel it into your character."

"Is it unhealthy that we want to leverage mental stress as a performance tactic?"

She winked at me. "That's showbiz, baby."

We laughed, and I felt a lightness settle in my chest where before there had been lead.

"Thank you," I said, sipping from the water.

"You're my stage husband," she said. "It's the least I could do."

I tried everything I could to make the second act go smoother, to find my balance, to hold my mental walls against my anxiety. I tried to imagine Mom in the crowd or in the sparkle of the lights, but all it did was make me aware of how many people were watching, of how hot I was in a wool suit being blasted by spotlights for hours.

When my character was accused of being a communist, I skipped my entire monologue defending myself, killing the emotional crescendo of the act. Instead, I sat down on a chair none of us had ever sat on before—and I believe that none of us were *supposed* to sit on—and delivered the final line of the monologue to allow Tyler to pick up his next line.

"Fine, drag me before a panel," I said, not having to act much to put the weariness in my voice.

It got worse as the next few scenes progressed. I found myself hiding more and more in that chair. It became my life raft in a sea of strange faces, the only thing keeping me in reality as the world shifted dangerously around me.

When it was time for me to pull a gun and shoot Tyler's character, I completely forgot about Angie's effects. Tyler and I carried off the scene like two school kids playing robbers together, with the gun motion happening and Tyler falling down wounded, but no gunshot sounds—until I sat back down.

The effects went off late and the ensuing gunshot effect made me topple over backwards in surprise, taking the chair with me as it split with a horrendous crack.

The audience roared in laughter at what was meant to be a very serious—and if done correctly, heart wrenching—scene.

And now we were short a set piece that I knew the crew had spent days chasing down from Berkeley. Their sister theatre would not be pleased we'd destroyed it.

When we took our bows, it was with no small amount of relief. Despite their polite applause, the audience seemed as relieved as we were to be done with the whole thing.

But they got to go home. We didn't.

The curtain fell but we weren't even off the stage before a familiar voice rang out, irritation carrying it across the rafters.

"What the *hell* was that?" Paul Vladik stormed across the stage directly toward me. "You're the biggest name in Hollywood for 8 years, and you can't deliver a few lines on a stage? How much editing went into those stupid movies?" He stopped only a few inches from me, and I could see he was quivering, a fine layer of sweat misted across his face.

"Chris is a talented actor." Nicole was still holding my hand after the bow. "He just had a rough night."

"A rough *opening* night," Paul spat. "Which, after all the chaos he brought here with the paparazzi and screwing the crew and pushing my nephew out of work, was also a rough *press preview*." A vein was pulsing in his forehead, but even as his rage slammed into me, something he'd said gave me pause.

Nicole opened her mouth to defend me, but I shot her a look. No one else needed to get taken down with me.

"I take full responsibility for what happened tonight," I said. "But, I'm afraid I'm not familiar with—"

"You should," he cut me off. "Because it's your fault. It's your fault the production ran so behind they're still having timing issues, and it's your fault this dramatic classic got turned into a slapstick routine because you couldn't keep your head on straight."

He was so angry his face was deep purple, and I worried he would explode like those old fruit candy commercials, brightly colored juice exploding across every surface.

"Alan," he whipped around. "Please tell me there's an understudy."

"There is, but—"

"No buts. Whoever they are, put them in. I'd rather have a nobody lead the show than this famous wreck."

"Who is your nephew?" Sarah's voice cut above the panicked murmurs and whispers.

"Who the fuck are you?" Paul glowered, spittle flying as he peered around the cast and crew, trying to find the source of the voice that was questioning him.

"Sarah Aguilar. I work here, sir." She stepped forward, hands planted firmly on her hip. "You said Chris put your nephew out of work. Who is it?"

Dawning realization drew gasps from across the stage, as if the sun itself had risen above that beautiful, *beautiful* woman and cast the shadows out with its brilliance.

"Leon, obviously. What does it matter?"

The murmurs turned to full frothing chatter, rising to a clattering din. It felt like everyone else's words were going to pull me under when only *one* thing truly mattered.

"Give me another chance, sir," I said, hating how much I felt like I was begging, how much I felt he was right. "Give me another chance to show I can still make great art."

A murmur of agreement rose up around us.

"Give you one more chance?" Paul whirled around, eyes bulging from his head.

"Uh, sir?" Angie called out from the wings.

"I don't know where you've been you think you can mess up *that* badly and still get to keep working," Paul's voice rose as he stalked toward me. "But it won't happen in my theatre ever again."

"Sir, really—" Angie kept trying.

"We strive for excellence Mister Hollywood, and whatever trash you think you can peddle on this stage is better off on the curb, where it belongs."

The curtain swung open, revealing the stunned audience staring straight at all of us. They must've heard yelling and thought maybe the show wasn't over. Whatever the reason, nearly 400 pairs of eyes were trained directly on Paul and me. We all stood there, silent, frozen to the spot.

I couldn't help feeling satisfied as the blood drained from Paul's face, his shoulders curving in protectively around his chest.

"Ladies and Gentlemen," Sarah's voice rang from the back of the stage, and the cast parted like the red sea for her to step to the front. "Thank you for your patience and grace on our opening night. As you may know, we've experienced some unique setbacks that impacted our production timelines."

Paul was glaring at her but kept his mouth shut.

"On top of that, our lead experienced a mental health event that prevented him from offering you his best this evening." A few gasps and understanding sounds went up across the House. Sarah nodded knowingly. "We've all been there." Scattered applause rang out in agreement.

"We'd like to ask you all return tomorrow night, on us, to give the show, and Chris, another chance. You won't be disappointed."

Much heartier applause than we'd received for the performance rang out and Sarah made several "thank you" gestures with her hands.

"Keep your tickets and simply bring them tomorrow, the rest will be handled for you," she called out, waving with her arms wide as the crowd finally began to filter out from the seats.

When she turned around, the friendly look on her face dropped immediately and she glared at Paul. That look was enough to convince me she could handle any backlash from the Box Office thanks to her generous offer.

"This time, wait until the House is cleared to start ripping anyone a new one," she hissed.

Sarah

It took some convincing but eventually Paul and Alan agreed to my plan.

Dorian arrived to distract Paul with some other crisis, and Alan gave out quick notes before sending everyone home to try and sleep things off.

Chris and I both passed out before we could talk about anything, with his gentle snoring lulling me into a deep sleep. Neither of us moved until the next morning.

I'd done plenty of openings but somehow this one drained me more than usual. Maybe it was all the worrying leading up to it that hadn't lessened during. In fact, I'd worried more during than I had before. Watching Chris crumble under anxiety was horrible. I'd felt so helpless.

"Hey," I said, throwing an exhausted arm across Chris' chest. He rubbed it lazily, grunting at me in response. "We told Betty we'd come for coffee today."

It was mid-morning, but it felt like 6:00 AM.

"No," he said, pouting.

"Yes," I said, rolling over to kiss his cheek before pushing myself out of bed. "I'll shower first, and then we should get moving. It's late already."

I stared at my reflection in the mirror while I waited for the shower to heat up.

Chris didn't know what I'd done when I left him at the deli the day before. I just hoped Betty would keep our secret.

I took my time in the shower, letting the hot water bring life back into my tired body, inhaling the steam. When I emerged, I felt almost human. The next step was coffee.

Chris was still in bed. I leaned over him, kissing his forehead before nudging him roughly. "Come on, your turn," I said. But he looped a clever hand around my arm and hauled me back into bed with him.

"You smell too good to get up yet," he said, grinning at me mischievously as he kissed me. I let him pull me back to the bed, relished his eager hands stripping me free of the towel as he rolled me onto my back. His tongue laved lazy circles over my still-wet breasts, taking his time on each nipple until I was arching into him, desperate for more. When he slid a finger into me, I was already wet. I swatted his hand away, grabbing his hips and shoving his boxers down with urgency.

Chris slid into me to his hips, and we moaned in unison at the connection. I pushed against him, turning us so that I straddled him now. I didn't have a headboard to help me balance, so I settled for slamming my palms against the wall, riding his cock as I chased my orgasm.

He slid warm hands up and down my back, urging me along when he reached my hips, looking up at me through a hazy, half-lidded gaze, a charming flush across his cheeks. I felt him lift me and I helped him, following his guidance to rise up and grind back down on his shaft, the slick, hot place between us reconnecting each time with a maddening pop. The force of it had me seeing stars, gravity plunging Chris deeper in me than before, a subtle discomfort urging me on. I wanted him deeper still, and I chased that need, no longer following his hands on my hips but rising and slamming all my own, faster and faster.

All too soon, the heat in my core twisted and ignited, and I came, crashing over the edge with a cry, slamming my hands against the wall again and again, not caring who heard.

I collapsed on top of Chris who stroked along my spine until I came back to myself from where my brain and heart had been catapulted to the stars.

Chris rolled me gently onto the bed, releasing himself from my pussy and pressing a quick kiss to my forehead before he left for the shower.

We were both flushed and happy as we made our way down the hall, a brief few minutes later.

Before we could knock, Betty's door swung wide.

"There are the happy lovers!" she cooed, ushering us both in and closing the door behind us.

The apartment smelled smokey and dark, like a vintage speakeasy. Light filtered in through drawn blinds, sparking the dust in the air with a new life and landing across shelves on the walls filled with knick-knacks and wilted paperbacks. Surprisingly, Gerald was nowhere to be seen.

"He plays dominoes on Saturdays," Betty said when I asked. "He'll be gone for the rest of the day."

As we settled on Betty's couch, she brought us chipped mugs filled with thick, dark coffee that consumed the cream I swirled into it. Chris took a sip and winced.

Betty laughed. "Café Cubano," she said.

I sipped with delight, letting the sweet, creamy beverage warm my throat on the way down. "It's got sugar in it already," I said to Chris. "You should give it more than one sip."

"I can make you something else?" Betty started to stand back up, ready to abandon her own beverage in favor of her hostess duties.

Chris waved her back into her seat shaking his head. "It's wonderful, I was just surprised is all."

"So," she said, leaning forward, a smile splitting her wrinkles. "Tell me about making movies, Chris."

I watched as he launched into story after story about being on set, doing his own stunts, and being starstruck while making a fool of himself. After a while, Betty's eyes grew misty and she leaned back, putting a hand over her mouth.

"I'm sorry," she said, sniffling. "But I was just thinking about how proud Mary would be."

Chris set his mug down and looked at his empty hands before looking up at Betty through the fringe of his hair.

"You have no idea how much it means to me to hear you say that."

The two reached across, holding hands for a moment. Betty was the first to let go, wiping under her eyes and shaking her head.

"Forgive us, Sarah," she said. "Sitting here weeping like a couple of old ladies."

I smiled. "I don't mind at all," I said. "I feel like I'm learning so much about Chris by just being here."

I leaned forward, giving Betty my best mischievous smile. "He promised me you'd have some embarrassing stories about him when he was younger."

Now it was Betty's turn, her face lighting up as she told me about Chris scaling the fire escape, sneaking out in high school, and the one time he convinced the building to put on a community production of Twelfth Night where he played half the cast himself.

"No one else wanted to be Malvolio," Chris said, laughing so hard he was bent over. "But I *really* wanted to be Sebastian."

"And apparently also the Duke and the twin sister," Betty said, and we all burst into more laughter together. "Give me a moment, I think I have photos."

"How is today?" I asked when we were alone.

"So much better now," he said. "And thank you for last night. You helped so much."

"It was a team effort," I said.

"Nicole is just my stage wife," he said, giving me a serious look. "Offstage it's all Sarah all the time."

"She's your stage wife, and I'm your backstage wife?" I said laughing.

Chris' face grew thoughtful. My heart skipped a beat. I'd just called myself his *wife*. Why did I like it?

"I'm so teasing," I said, holding my hand up between the two of us, desperate to recover. "I'm your girlfriend, no wife talk yet. Or at all. Ever, even we don't have to—"

"Here it is," Betty held the album aloft as she returned, saving me from myself.

She handed it me and Chris, letting us page through at our own pace. There was a young Betty in the 60s, standing in front of our apartment building with a brilliant, proud smile. There she was smoking in a bar, a posh cocktail dangling from the other hand. Time passed as we flipped the pages, and soon enough, halfway through, there was a shy, blonde toddler peering up at the camera from Betty's lap.

I stopped and pointed, looking at Betty questioningly and she nodded.

"That was the first week you lived here," she said. "Mary came by to introduce herself once the dust was settled, and she brought you with her. You were too shy to talk yet, but you crawled right in my lap looking for some loving."

"You were a *cute* baby!" I gasped.

A few more pages, and I watched Chris grow up before my eyes, tucked between photos of Betty's furniture sets and laughing neighbors.

There was Mary, holding Chris' hand in the same hall we walked every day, offering half a tired smile to the camera. Chris was turned away, the early teen years setting in, the collar flipped up on his denim jacket.

Finally, there was Mary, beaming proudly from under her son's arms as he held up his first playbill. He was taller than she was in the photo, Mary's brunette bob barely brushing his shoulder. But the two looked happier than I'd seen any two people in a photograph.

"Oh yes," Betty said when we lingered in silence on that photo for longer than the others. "You remember that day, I'm sure, Chris."

He nodded.

"That was the first show I did at CAT."

"Betty," I asked. "Can I borrow this photo? I'd like to scan it and share it with the theatre. They'd love to have it for the archives."

"Even after last night?" Chris closed the album and handed it back to Betty. She quickly flipped the pages back open, loosening the photo from its corners and handing it to me. It came loose much easier than I imagined the other photos would. I hoped Chris wouldn't notice.

"One bad show isn't going to make Alan erase you from the theatre's history," I said.

"I wasn't talking about Alan," he muttered.

"Something happened last night?" Betty asked.

"We had a rough opening," I said. "That's all."

"I can't do theatre anymore, Mrs. Normandy," he said. "That's what Sarah isn't telling you."

"You always were a little overdramatic," Betty said, settling back into her seat. "You came home after you flunked a math quiz one day, screaming down the hall about how you were too stupid for school, and you'd never amount to anything."

"Woah, dude," I said, giving Chris a teasing look.

"I don't know where all that pressure you put on yourself came from," Betty said. "Mary would've worshipped the ground you walked on whether you were walking it in the shoes of a car mechanic, a movie star, or a hobo."

Chris sighed and ran a hand through his hair. "I didn't want to let her down."

"It would've been impossible anyway," Betty said. "I *know* she's proud of you now, coming home when it's hardest, getting back up on stage after all this time."

"I just wish she was here," Chris said, voice trembling.

"She is, sweet boy," Betty said. "She is."

When we got to the theatre that night, there was a line around the block. Apparently, the reviews for opening night had slammed Paul for belittling an actor who was clearly in need of increased mental health support. If San Francisco was one thing, it was a place filled to the brim with people dying to demonstrate how politically correct they could be compared to the rest of the world.

An actor wasn't going to have a panic attack on a San Francisco stage and be left to suffer, that was for sure.

"Are they really all here for the show?" Chris asked as he waved and smiled before we ducked into the side entrance. There were so many potential audience members, the paparazzi had been chased across the street.

"I did promise everyone from last night a free redo," I said. "I hope they all fit without the Fire Marshall getting called."

Inside, there was a fresh energy backstage that had been missing the night before. Everyone was fired up after Paul's tirade. Marisol was clipping threads and tightening waists at a rate I'd never seen in my life, and the prop master was standing guard over his table with a long, thick ruler, smacking any hands that wandered too close.

Even Angie was on a roll, firing blast after blast to ensure they really would go off correctly this time.

"I switched the tape," she said. "Less adhesive to burn through, should fix the timing." There was soot all over her face and her left eyebrow was singed.

We were going to give the best show anyone had ever seen, or we were going to die trying.

"5 minutes to showtime," Alan called out. Feet scrambled, breaths caught, Chris kissed me squarely on the mouth as he passed me, letting Nicole guide him to their places.

The curtain pulled back, and we held our breath, collectively.

Miracle of miracles, tonight's audience and last night's audience fit into the House, but that meant it was packed beyond full. Dorian shoved folding chairs into every spare corner of the house, and James and Greg were stationed to deal with any rule-mongers who might try to shut the whole thing down.

I let out a slow exhale, tuning into my headset and focusing on the show. My surprise for Chris was finally in place after a delay at the shop.

All I could do now was wait and hope.

CHRIS

Tonight was already going smoother. Even though the audience was doubled from last night, I was able to throw myself into Harry, forgetting that anyone was watching us at all. I was no longer Chris Oldfelds, screen actor returning to the stage, I was Harry Stratford, whose only worry was keeping his wife safe from the feds.

When we got to the dreaded kitchen scene, Nicole and I carried it off flawlessly. This time we weren't even thinking about the lines—we were thinking about whether or not Harry was having an affair, whether or not Nicole was clever enough to figure it out.

Finally, here were the tracks our train needed, and we were firmly on them.

When the curtain closed for Act Two, those of us standing on stage leapt into a chaotic group hug, limbs flailing and knees knocking together. Nicole kissed my cheek. Tyler smacked my back good-naturedly.

"Good work everyone," Alan called as we filed backstage. "Don't lose that energy."

Sarah found me, leaping into my arms and wrapping herself entirely around me.

"Do you hear the crowd?" she squealed. "They're gasping and ooing and awing! They're so in it!"

"I haven't heard anything," I said, blissed out. "I'm in the zone, Sarah, it's like no one's even there."

"Oh, someone's there," she said, giving me a knowing wink as I set her back down on the ground.

"Stop being happy and gross," Angie came over, swatting us both playfully.

"That's the first time you've announced your arrival," Sarah said, grinning at her best friend.

"I didn't want to scare Chris," she said, grinning. "I figured it would be better to save my cat-like graces for another day."

"Chris thanks you," I said, returning her teasing.

"Five minutes to curtain," Alan called out. I heard the bell dinging distantly, meaning the guests would be returning to their seats.

"Break every limb," Sarah said. I scooped her into a kiss I wished I didn't have to break, stepping back out onto the stage.

Again, we were in our groove, moving through each emotional beat of each scene. I delivered my monologue, making sure to leave the emotional crescendo to the end, finishing to impromptu scattered applause.

I can do this, I thought to myself as we transitioned to the next scene.

But then it was time for the gunshots. A certain tension thickened over the stage. I couldn't stop myself from glancing to where the chair, now in pieces in the back, had sat.

Tyler delivered his line. I raised my prop gun. We'd done this a thousand times before. This was just once more.

"It'll snow in Florida before you take me alive," I said, delivering the cue line for Angie's explosives.

A horrifying silence stretched between us.

"It'll snow in Florida before you take me alive," I said again, this time louder, punctuating each word as aggressively as I could.

Tyler and I locked eyes, unsure if we should keep moving through the scene or wait for the explosives. Last night, we hadn't waited, and the shock of them had disrupted us further.

My chest tightened. My breath came in short, sharp gasps.

Not again. I lowered the gun and focused on my breathing, hoping it looked like my character was really struggling with whether or not to shoot Tyler's character.

Spots appeared in the corners of my eyes. I prayed I wouldn't pass out.

Somehow, Sarah's voice came to me through the panicked fog.

Can you visualize your mom in the crowd? She'd asked me last night. I took another deep breath, carefully turning my head to glance out into the crowd.

And then I stopped breathing altogether.

There, standing in the aisle as if by some otherworldly miracle, was my mom. She was wearing the same dress she'd worn to my first play in this very theatre, and she looked so happy I nearly burst into tears at the sight.

She was here.

I turned back to Tyler, pointing the prop gun back up and to the right of him, a precautionary detail even if there weren't blanks in the gun.

"You capitalist monsters can't even make bullets correctly," I snarled. And then the effect went off and Tyler dropped expertly, as if that was the moment he'd been waiting for this entire time.

That guy may have started as an understudy, but he was leading now.

A gasp echoed around the audience. We finished the scene.

The rest of the act passed in a half-imagined blur, some part of me lost to Harry Stratford, the other soaking in the energetic crowd.

Finally, the curtain pulled on the tragic ending.

When we came out for curtain call, the crowd was ecstatic, nearly 800 voices screaming and applauding and whistling.

Tears fell as I took my bow. I couldn't help it. It was such a relief to finally perform well, to have conquered my sudden onslaught of stage fright, and to have my mom witness it all, however impossible that seemed.

I looked out into the audience again as we joined hands to take the group bow and there she still was, beaming out at me.

I barely made it on stage long enough for the curtain to finally close on us, sprinting backstage and through the side door that would take me to the House.

I had to see how this was possible, had to see if she was real.

I jostled my way through the slow filter of guests leaving the House, accepting congratulations and trying to decline requests for selfies as kindly as I could.

When I made it to the aisle, my mom was still there but there was something different than the vision I'd seen from the stage. She didn't appear as clearly or as brightly as she had from a distance. And that's when I saw it—a cardboard triangle protruding from her back, propping her up.

It was my mom—a photo of her, blown up to life-size scale and placed in the aisle so it looked as if she were watching me.

"I hope it's okay." Sarah's voice came from behind me. She was walking up the vom from the orchestra pit. "It's the only way I could figure out to have her be here for you."

"It's perfect," I whispered, staring at her in awe. The stage lights were bouncing off her dark curls, giving her an illuminated halo, and it was all I could do not to fall to my knees for the incredible kindness she'd shown me.

Actually, suddenly my knees didn't seem like such a bad idea. Or at least one of them didn't.

Without thinking, I dropped to a knee, taking Sarah's hands in mine.

"What're you doing?" She whispered, face turning beet red as she looked around at the still crowded theatre.

"I don't have a ring," I said. "But what you've done for me tonight is wife behavior. Not stage wife, not backstage wife, just *wife* behavior."

"I didn't think you'd like it that much," she said, eyes wide, face stretched in surprised.

"Sarah Aguilar, I want you to marry me. At some point."

"You're skipping steps, drama queen." But she was smiling so wide I could've fallen into it, letting her joy drown me. "I think there's something important we should say to each other first."

"I love you." I leapt to my feet, snatching Sarah off the ground and whirling her around in my arms, unable to stop and think, not wanting to. "I love you, I love you, I love you."

"Your turn!" Someone yelled from on stage. I was suddenly aware of the entire audience around us, the cast and crew peeking out from behind the curtain.

"Oh shit," I breathed, setting Sarah down and gesturing to the keenly invested eyes on us.

"Well?" An older woman in a lilac suit looked at Sarah. "If you don't keep him, I might scoop him up, young lady."

"I hope you won't break my heart, ma'am," Sarah answered. "I'm pretty in love with him."

SARAH

Chris took me to pick out a ring the following Monday. I told him he didn't have to. Honestly, I almost didn't want to. It seemed like yet another thing for people to accuse me of gold-digging.

But when I called my mom to tell her the good news, and her first question was "Qué anillo, mija?" I felt an ache in my chest.

I hadn't given much thought to getting married. I'd always imagined my life with a partner of some kind, happily dedicated to each other regardless of the legal promise we made. But when Chris dropped to one knee in the theatre that night, my gut knew.

I mean, it really *knew* that this was what I wanted.

So, I decided if I was listening to my gut, and my gut said to get a ring in the face of the naysayers, then that's what we would do.

Chris suggested Tiffany's and Cartier, begging me to let him spend of his hard-earned movie money on something that wasn't massive takeout orders for our fellow crewmembers.

I let him guide me through the polished and brightly lit shops in Union Square, feeling wildly out of place and overwhelmed. Each store had an identical saleswoman with a high sleek ponytail and flaw-less makeup. They only made eye contact with Chris and asked what *he* wanted, what *he* liked. They showed him diamonds the size of a quarter. I felt sick to my stomach.

Each time, Chris turned to me, eyes questioning. Each time I shook my head and tried to fight off the dizzy spell threatening to topple me.

Finally, after several high-end stores, we stopped for coffee, sitting in the square and watching the pigeons heckle tourists taking selfies in the rare sunshine.

"I think we should skip the whole ring thing," I said finally, rein-vigorated by the caffeine and dreading stepping into yet another flu-orescent Thunderdome.

"It's whatever you want," he said, eyeing me over his cup. "I thought you wanted a ring, but you seem really uncomfortable. Is it too fast? We can always do this later."

"No one's asking me for my opinion on anything. They're only talking to you and all of the rings are *huge*," I sighed. "It's overwhelm-ing, I'm sorry. I don't want to seem ungrateful or like I'm not excited. It's just too much."

Chris considered me, his head cocked to the side. Then he stood, taking my hand and hauling me up with him.

"I've got an idea," he said.

Back in our neighborhood, he led me past the deli and through a parklet I swore hadn't been there a week ago. On the other side, nestled between corner stores and Vietnamese restaurants, was a narrow little shop with a few glinting pieces in the window. The sign above the door read "Charm Bros. Jewelry" in gold, hand-painted letters. We had to press a call button to be buzzed in through the floor-to-ceiling iron-barred door.

The shop stretched to the back in one long narrow hall, with a jewelry counter on one side. The pieces on display were beautiful: delicate gold wristwatches, earrings made from perfectly imperfect freshwater pearls, and necklaces that looked like something from a safe on the Titanic. But I gasped when we reached the ring case.

Amethysts, emeralds, and rubies sparkled up at me, but these were different from the identical flawless cuts we'd been staring at for the last several hours. Something about them felt welcoming, calling out to me from the case.

An older Black man appeared from the back, waving to us both and moving slowly to the ring case.

"Hello, hello," he said, wiping polish off his hands and onto his apron. He stopped when he saw Chris. We braced for the usual "hey, you're famous" routine that had become a part of us being in public these days.

"Are you Mary's kid?" he asked. Chris slowly nodded, offering the man a half smile.

"I am," he said. "But I'm sorry, I don't think I know you."

The man shook his head. "You wouldn't," he said. "You were little when she brought you with her, but you have her cheeks and her smile. I'd recognize that smile anywhere."

"How'd you know my mom?" Chris asked, looking around the shop for some clue.

"It wasn't under the best of circumstances," he said. "I'm not sure she'd want you to know."

"You know, don't you?" Chris asked and I slipped my hand in his, hoping it fortified the news he was about to deliver.

The man took one look at our faces and bowed his head, letting out a slow exhale. He nodded slowly when he looked back up at us.

"I'm sorry for your loss," he said. "But I think I might have something that will help."

We waited in silence, Chris' palm sweating against mine.

"We don't have to do this," I finally said. "Really, let's go home and finish our Kenneth Branagh marathon."

Chris shook his head. "It's alright," he said. "I want to see what magic this guy has up his sleeve."

The man returned with a ring box, the edges worn with time. He opened it carefully, the tiny hinges shrieking in protest. I gasped again, putting a hand across my mouth as warmth bloomed in my chest.

Inside was a delicate white gold band holding a single square-cut ruby. The setting was secure but not obtrusive, leaving you to enjoy the gem's presence by itself. On either side, nestled against the ruby, were two tiny diamonds, winking at me in the shop's soft light.

"Try it on," the man said, something making his voice thick.

The ring slid on with no protest—a perfect fit.

"Wow," I said, holding my hand up to admire it. The stones gleamed, the band was soft. It hardly felt like I was wearing anything at all but there it was, nestled against my skin as if it were made to be there. "It's perfect."

I showed Chris who immediately teared up. I was hitching myself to a real crybaby.

"It *is* perfect," he said. He glanced back to the man. "But I'm sorry, as much as I love it, I don't understand what it has to do with my mom."

"It was hers," the man said simply. "She came sold it to me a long time ago. Said she needed to pay some registration fee for her kid's theatre camp."

"I had no idea," Chris breathed.

"That was probably on purpose," the man said.

"And you kept it all this time?" I asked in disbelief.

"Oh god no," he laughed. "I tried to sell it. But it fell out of fashion and just sat in the case. Eventually I switched it out for other things, but something wouldn't let me just give it away or melt it down. I tend to have a good nose for these things, so I held on to it. Lucky you." He grinned at us both.

"We'll take it, obviously," I said before turning to Chris. "If that's okay."

"Whatever you want," he said, smiling softly.

"Including your late-mom's ring?" I asked, arching my eyebrows.

"If it's what *you* want," he said, arching his eyebrows back at me.

"I can't really explain it, Chris," I said, glancing down at the ring again. "It's perfect. I don't want to take it off."

"And you took all the others off pretty fast," he said smiling. "It was meant to be."

He looked to the man behind the counter and pulled out his wallet, but the man waved his hands in dismissal.

"Absolutely not," he said. "Your mom was doing what she had to, just like we all do at some point. I'm glad the ring found its family again."

The two argued about whether or not Chris would pay the man and finally they agreed that he would pay back what the man had given his mom for the ring nearly 15 years ago: $65.65.

When we stepped back out onto the street, I looped my arm through Chris' and nearly skipped back toward the apartment.

"Are you happy?" he asked, grinning down at me.

"Ecstatic," I said. "Thank you." He kissed me on the corner before we crossed the street.

"You know the best part?" I asked. "We don't have a show tonight. We can do *whatever* we want." I waggled my eyebrows at him suggestively.

"I want to buy you a new dress and take you to the most ridiculously expensive dinner the city has," he said, waggling his eyebrows back.

"Chris, that's not—"

"Necessary, blah blah," he finished for me, teasingly. "But I want to. And you won't let me buy you a big, fat diamond to show off with so let me do this."

"Alright," I said, rolling my eyes but smiling so hard I thought my face might crack in half. "Let's go shopping, twist my arm."

CHRIS

Weeks later, and closing night sunk its teeth into me. I could barely believe the show was ending, leaving a massive gap for new beginnings. I'd have to find an apartment in the city, start my life here anew.

Sarah had disappeared into rehearsals, with her show opening the following week. We hadn't seen each other more than to fall in bed exhausted each night and I missed her. I couldn't believe I already missed her.

It cemented for me that the surprise I was planning for Sarah was right. It was more than a thank you for the ones she'd already given me. It was, I hoped, a promise of all the surprises we would keep giving each other for the rest of our lives. I'd already bought out the entire front row of her first performance, filling it with friends and family—the same friends and family I hoped would come tonight.

I had been purposefully vague about what would happen at the show, simply saying it was for both Sarah and I, and that it would be the surprise of a lifetime.

That was enough to get people to agree to be there.

Getting in touch with Sarah's family in the East Bay had taken some finagling—mostly telling Angie all the juicy details in exchange for a short list of phone numbers and names. She was sworn to secrecy, but I still hadn't slept the night after, carefully tucking the list into the back of my wallet where I knew Sarah wouldn't find it.

The hardest part was getting Sarah to be in the theatre for closing night. She'd wanted to watch, finally set loose from her backstage duties in favor of rehearsing her new role on a tight schedule. But I needed her backstage so she could be onstage when the curtain fell.

Somehow, Angie worked it out so Sarah's replacement suffered a last-minute injury, and she called Sarah in tears, pleading with her to come do the final show so that things could continue to run as smooth as they had since we found our groove that second night.

I didn't want to know if Angie was responsible or if the injury was fake. That woman scared me a little.

Sarah, of course, had agreed. Anything to help.

I shoved everything from my mind as I took my mark on the stage for the opening scene of our final show together.

Well, not quite final.

Alan had already offered me a long-term position with the company, having stepped into Paul's recently vacated role as Interim Artistic Director, saying he'd find a role within the current season if I took the offer. But he'd also suggested that I take some time off and focus on starting my new life with my fiancé.

"You've worked hard for a long time," he said. "And Sarah is starting something bold and beautiful. She'll need your support to weather the uglier parts of it."

I knew I'd be back on the stage before too long, but Alan was right. I wanted to be there for my fiancé.

Soon to be wife, I thought to myself as the curtain rose and the lights came up.

\#

My nerves vibrated through me with every scene we finished, drawing closer and closer to final curtain—and the big reveal.

My nerves began to jangle, vibrating through me with every scene we finished, drawing closer and closer to the end of the show and the big reveal.

Sarah was in the wings, ensuring things moved smoothly with no idea what was about to happen. What if she hated what I'd planned? What if she was embarrassed? What if this ended everything?

High risk, high reward—or so I'd been told.

Hands found me in the dark as I exited the stage for the second intermission. A familiar scent, the press of soft curls, and a voice that sent heat trailing long fingers down my spine.

"I've missed you." I kissed Sarah back, all-too-aware of the silent comings and going in the wings, the rustling of the curtains around us as set pieces, costumes, and wigs were all reset, stripped, primped, and preened for the final act.

Her hands slid down my torso, tracing lazy circles until she found my cock.

"*Sarah.*" I growled against her mouth, grinding into her touch. "We could get caught." *Fuck, that's hot.*

"Just a little something to think about for later." I could feel her warmth slipping away. I groped through the dark, catching her just in time and hauling her back against me.

"Fuck later," I said, capturing her mouth and devouring her.

We were a mess of hasty, trembling limbs, shoving aside shirts, tugging at pants, desperate for the skin we couldn't see, tangled in the deep dark of the wings where not even veteran crew could find us.

I cupped Sarah's breasts, groaning into her mouth at the hard buds that pushed back against my palms, feeling her own hard arousal as she worked my dick from my pants. She barely had her gorgeous lips wrapped around my length before I looped my arms through hers and hauled her up to my waist. Sarah wrapped her legs around me as we both frantically shoved her work pants down. Holding her to me with one arm wrapped iron tight on her lower back, I slid my free hand into her pussy, practically coming undone at how wet she was for me.

"Has anyone seen Chris?" A hoarse voice whispered in the dark. Dissenting murmurs, pattering shoes, more rippling curtains. We were running out of time.

"Ready?" I whispered.

"God, yes," Sarah gasped back. I wanted to see her throwing her head back, wanted to study the arch of her neck, the shape of her lips as she said my name. But for now, we needed the dark, needed each other.

"Chris?" A second whisper sought me out as I thrust into Sarah. Her soft fingers clamped over my mouth, smothering my groan at the perfect fit. I nipped at her fingertips as she ground against me, taking me to the hilt. I lifted her just enough for her to slam herself back onto me, gripping my shoulders and shaking at the exertion, her lips replacing her fingers to smother our cries as she slammed back again, and again, and again. Rhythm and desperation warred for dominance in our silent dance, more scurrying feet padding through the dark, more time ticking by, pushing us to race against the waning clock.

My orgasm grew brighter and brighter in the edges of my vision as Sarah worked her pussy over my slick cock, her movements getting faster, jerkier, more lost in her need than before. *Oh shit my costume. Fuck.*

"Come on, beautiful." I whispered against her ear, stroking her hair, supporting her plump ass. "You feel so good, keep going for me."

She rose and landed, hands bruising through my costume.

"Yes, just like that. Don't stop. You look so good riding me like that."

Her breath was hot on my face, hair a curtain around us, blocking anything else from occupying my limited vision.

"I love your pussy. *God.* I want to fuck you until you forget any name but mine."

Sarah kissed me then, a punishing crush of our mouths that I realized too late was her smothering her cries as she orgasmed. I felt her clenching around me, milking me, riding through the last shuddering waves of her release. I followed quickly behind, the heat and tightness of her enveloping me on all sides sending me over the edge.

When we were both spent and the world came back into sharp focus, I gently set her down on wobbly legs. I tucked myself into my pants—slowly and more carefully than I ever had before. I could *not* get semen on my costume and live to tell about it. Marisol was scarier than Angie. Sarah adjusted her crew uniform, both of us barely quick enough as a familiar voice chirped from the dark.

"Why does it smell like sex back here?"

"Jesus *Christ,* Angie!" Sarah shrieked. "And I dunno, was Tyler back here with the new PA? I saw them eyeballing each other earlier." She continued the casual gossip, luring Angie away my hiding spot.

I didn't miss the wink she gave before they disappeared further in the wings.

I was making a really good decision locking her in.

All too soon, we were in our curtain call formation, grabbing hands and bowing to thunderous applause.

"Ready?" Nicole asked, squeezing my hands as we straightened from a bow. I nodded. My heart was threatening to fall out of my mouth if I opened it.

"Ladies and Gentlemen," Nicole called. "We have a closing night celebration. We invite you all to stay for a final surprise here on the stage. Please remain in your seats."

A flurry of activity kicked off behind us as surprised murmurs rang out throughout the crowd. The strike crew moved with lightning speed and precision, tearing down the smaller set pieces and hauling in the small platform I'd requested. A few people came out with bouquets and stands to display them on as red silk drapes gracefully dropped from the ceiling. I saw Marisol loop an arm around Sarah's waist and drag her away before she could protest.

Tyler appeared at my side with the suit I'd ordered, helping me switch out jacket and shirt to an embarrassing amount of shrieks and whistles from the audience. A new electricity gripped the building as the orchestra retuned and formerly antsy audience members re-settled into their seats.

Angie appeared at my side, wearing a navy-blue dress that brushed the ground when she walked. She'd pinned her long hair up into a graceful sweep of a bob and small pearls clung to her ears.

"You look amazing!" I said. "I don't think I've ever seen you in anything other than your work clothes."

"That's on purpose," she deadpanned, reaching over and pinning a small lily to my lapel. "Ready?" she asked, offering her arm.

"That's my line." I grinned, taking it.

The orchestra struck up a romantic waltz as Angie and I stepped from the wings in unison with Mrs. Normandy and Tyler on the opposite side of the stage. My old neighbor wore a knee-length navy dress to match Angie, and had a lily pinned to her chest like I did. The four of us met each other in the center of the stage before breaking apart in a scramble of hugs. I stepped up onto the raised dais now surrounded by billowing waves of silk and fresh flowers from the sidewalk vendor down the street. I'd bought them out for the day, so we had every cut and variety that would normally draw in a potential buyer from passing by on their way to work.

It smelled heavenly, reminding me of rainy mornings in San Francisco on the way to catch the bus to school when my mom would stop and smell the flowers at the street stalls before hurrying on our way.

It was one more way to have her here with me.

Nicole and Alan came out next, meeting Marisol and the prop master before again breaking apart in a flurry of hugs and well-wishes.

There was no more waiting now.

The orchestra broke into a string rendition of I Left My Heart in San Francisco and the spotlight found Sarah at the back of the house. My heart leapt out of my throat as I caught sight of my soon-to-be wife.

Marisol had dressed her in white silk, draping it expertly around her body so that it hugged in all the right places before billowing out into a graceful train. Sarah wore white wrist-length gloves and clutched a bouquet of lilies to her chest. She'd skipped the veil, and Marisol had pinned flowers throughout Sarah's voluptuous curls that framed her face in a glowing halo.

Sarah walked down the house aisle to the stage, and by the time she reached me on the dais, I could see that tears were slowly rolling down her face. Angie reached over and took her bouquet. Our hands found each other.

"You can tell me if this is too much." Fear was pulling at my corners, but I refused it, relishing every glowing moment.

"You planned all this?" she asked, a smile splitting her face. "For me?"

"For us," I said, relief swelling in my chest.

"Thank you all for joining us tonight, for the union of Sarah Aguilar and Chris Oldfelds." James began. He, too, was dressed in navy, a lily on his lapel.

They'd been my mom's favorites.

"The couple has not prepared their own vows," James said. "Because the bride didn't know she'd be getting married tonight." The audience chuckled and a few hearty cheers rang out. Sarah laughed, looking out at the front row and mouthing something to her mom that made them both laugh.

"But I'm going to give them a minute to say something to each other anyway," he said, throwing me a wink. It was off script, and it was gutsy, but I liked it.

James handed me the mic.

"Sarah," I started, my voice shaking. "From the moment we met on this very stage I couldn't keep my eyes off you. Something about you felt right, and it wasn't until you slipped my mother's ring on your finger that I knew it was because *you* were right. You were right for me and for my life. You are exactly who I've been looking for without even knowing it, and I hope that we will keep each other for as long as we still fit."

I handed the mic to Sarah, dabbing at my eyes with the corner of my suit sleeve until Alan reached up and offered me his kerchief.

"Chris," she said between dramatic sniffles. Who knew we were both such criers? "You've made me believe I deserve so much more in this life than I would've thought possible. Your kindness and support have pushed me to achieve dreams I never thought would come true. I can't believe how lucky I am to be with you every day, and I hope we will keep each other for as long as we still fit."

She handed the mic back to James without breaking eye contact, her mascara smudged around her water line, her cheeks flushed with the tears she was holding back.

"Couldn't have said it more beautifully if it was written down," James said, earning a few more giggles from the crowd. I would need to ask him if he'd ever considered show biz before the night was over. He was a natural.

"And now, if the couple would repeat after me:"

He asked us if we would always choose each other. We said we would.

He asked us if we would always honor each other. We said we would.

He asked if we would do anything and everything to keep one another healthy, happy, sane, and sheltered for the rest of our lives.

We said we would.

"Well then, I won't make you wait any longer, buddy," James clapped a hand on my shoulder. "By the power invested in me by BeAMinister.Com, you may now kiss the bride."

Sarah threw her arms around me, hauling me into a deep, passionate kiss that maybe wasn't totally appropriate for the crowd gathered. Hoots and hollers rang out amid the thunderous applause and when we finally pulled apart, it was to a standing ovation.

I took our clasped hands and threw them aloft as if we'd just won the world series. Sarah waved and blew kisses to her family in the front row.

"The happy couple will now host a modest reception in the lobby. Please join us for wine, beer, and popcorn to celebrate our Sarah and Chris."

And we were theirs. As much as Sarah was mine, and I hers, this city, this theatre, held us both so entirely and completely, that we would never even consider going anywhere else in the world.

This was home, for better and for worse.

Epilogue: Sarah

I was huddled in front of the green room toilet, shivering. I hadn't vomited yet, but the bile rose in the back of my throat, a gurgling threat.

"Girl, you got like three minutes," Angie called through the door.

"Okay," I answered back, finally pushing myself up off the floor. Thankfully my costume was intact—no vomit, no drool, no sweat. But I was a mess.

"Yikes," Angie said as the door swung open.

"Not helping," I said, pulling on the large floppy hat that matched my dress.

"What if you're pregnant?" Angie continued.

"*Really* not helping," I said, trying to ignore her and making my weak-kneed way toward the stage.

"Well at least you'll have bigger things to think about than the packed house waiting for you out there."

"Angie," I snapped. "Go somewhere else."

"But I'm bored, I don't have—"

"Go. Somewhere. Else."

She rolled her eyes and stalked off.

"You're no fun anymore," she threw over her shoulder. I ignored it. Angie's particular brand of bluntness was not what I needed tonight of all nights.

My nerves had been trying to destroy me for the last few days as my first performance got closer and closer.

Staring down stepping on the stage for real, I had begun to wonder if I was the stupidest person on the planet. Why did I leave the safety of the wings for this specific type of torture?

Having crushed his debut in *Caught Red-Handed,* Tyler was offered the lead romantic role for *Company.* It was his smiling face that found me in the wings. He offered me his arm, looking painfully handsome in his tailored costume, and flashed me a winning smile.

"My fair lady," he said, giggling at his own joke.

"I'll throw up on you," I warned.

He stuck his tongue out at me. "I helped with three little sisters. Do your worst."

"I'm so scared," I whispered as he guided me gently to our marks on the stage.

"You've got all of us with you," Tyler whispered back. "And Chris bought out the whole front row."

I nodded, fortified thinking of my *husband* waiting for the curtain to pull back. The panic dissipated as I remembered I'd have at least one familiar set of eyes to look for if I got scared or stuck.

Chris had been amazing since his show closed—*of course* he had. The rave reviews got him several offers across the country—including New York—but he turned them all down. He was devoted to me during rehearsals, running lines with me in-between his cooking duties—which he had taken to with a gluttonous passion. When we had downtime, he arranged romantic dates to walk through museums during their quiet off hours or wandering through bookstores. One particularly gloomy Monday, he took me to a gourmet sweet shop where we tasted every type of black licorice made all around the world. I loved it. He spit it in the trash.

Chris had also been working with James, connecting him to open auditions and helping him prepare for each one. He really saw something in the guy, and I loved seeing him use his network to help other people realize their full potential.

And of course, there was the whole "wife thing." I still didn't quite know what it meant, to be Chris' life partner and equal person in all things. But I was more and more excited every day to figure it out.

Mami was already asking about nietos.

What if you're pregnant? Angie's joke rang through my head.

Amá *and* Angie.

I shook my head. The cat-like creeping weirdo of Contemporary American Theatre, SF, wanted me to have kids as bad as Mamí did. I regretted letting them drink together at our surprise wedding.

Maybe it was time to hook Angie up with a distraction. I considered Tyler in the lowlight of the stage while the introductory theme for the show rang out from the orchestra pit. Angie didn't really have a type, but Tyler was handsome, kind, and talented. Maybe it was worth a shot.

But I didn't have time to think about anyone or anything else as the curtain raised and the lights found us, spotlighting us in the dark.

Tyler's voice rang out strong and sure across the audience, and I clung to those notes for comfort as my own voice rose to meet his.

This was it.

My heart was pounding, and I almost couldn't hear the orchestra over the rush of blood in my ears. My wiggling legs followed Tyler's sure stride across the stage as he led me through the blocking we'd practiced together thousands of times.

I was immediately grateful I couldn't make out faces directly due to the angle of the lights on the stage. I was sure if I knew too many people looking at me that closely, I'd combust on the spot.

I was having trouble slipping into my character, as much as I wished I could hide. I was sure I looked as nervous as I felt—which was *not* cute.

Too late, I realized I'd been lost in thought and the orchestra was holding for my entrance to the next song. It was my solo, even.

I felt panic claw up my throat with needle-like claws, cutting off my every attempt to open my mouth and sing.

I was going to go down before I'd even begun to rise.

"Chris," Tyler mouthed, catching my eye and nodding toward the audience.

This was our agreed upon emergency tactic if I froze up on stage during a performance. Chris would be in an obvious place in the audience, letting me see him when I looked out.

I tried it, panic clenching my chest tighter as I waited for my eyes to adjust.

There, in the front row, smack center of the stage, was my husband. And he wasn't wearing anything except his underwear. In fact, no one in the front row—all our friends and family—was wearing real clothes. They were *all* in their underwear.

I cracked a smile, stepping back a little until they faded to a glow again, and I nodded to the conductor.

He counted me in a final time with the introductory measures and this time, when I opened my mouth, a song rose out.

I felt myself sink into the character, a woman who only wanted to be loved and safe in a world that wished her anything but. She sang about the fear and terror she carried in her heart, and about how desperately she wished this handsome man would assuage those things in her. Yet she knew only she could ease her own fears.

It wasn't hard to find the motivation for the song when I'd lived it so clearly.

When the song finished, the audience erupted before Tyler had a chance to say his next line. I let the applause wash over me, finding my place next to my costar and waiting for things to die down long enough for us to continue.

I'd done it. I'd started. And now I would *never* stop. I was the happiest I'd ever been, the closest to my dream life I had ever come, and I had already started dreaming of new and wondrous things to chase next.

And I could *not* wait.

ACKNOWLEDGEMENTS

I wrote the original draft of Songbird in a single week—largely just to see if I could. It was a humbling exercise, early in my romance author career, where I learned how much physical and mental work goes into making two people fall convincingly in love. I shelved the draft after it's initial rejections from traditional publishers, letting Sarah and Chris percolate in the back of my mind. I am first and foremost, grateful to that back burner and to the other writers I know who taught me it's okay to leave a draft alone for a little while. Without that time to breathe, *Songbird* wouldn't be what it is. I'm grateful to my ever-present writing partners, Britta and Molly, who gave endless feedback on multiple revisions over several years to help me bring *Songbird* to life. As always, I am nothing without my sisters—Amber and Jacqueline who forever feed the inspiration for the fierce women in my stories. Thank you to Amanda Webb for her gorgeous artwork that brings Chris and Sarah to life, and to my sensitivity reader who shall remain anonymous, for calling me in with sharp and careful critique. Thank you to my husband, for sweeping me off my feet in every restaurant across the Bay Area, small, huge, dingy, white-linens, local, high-end, Michelin Star, or Bib Gourmand—it never matters, so long as we dine together.

But really, truly—maybe self-indulgently—I am grateful to my past self. Little 25-year-old Kel Bruem scraping through the most expensive part of the country, alone, scared, determined, and covered in mental bugs. Without her, I wouldn't be where I am today: safe, loved, soaring.

Thank you, reader, for following me this far, and I hope we'll get to adventure together again soon.

Also by Kel Bruem

What's Luck Got to Do With It

rumpy/Sunshine, He Falls First, Hidden Identities, Forbidden Love, He Has How Many Eggplants?!, Meddling Best Friends, Secret Societies, Boston in the Fall

Caiomhe Ryan is the luckiest girl in Boston—she has a great job, a cute apartment, and a ride-or-die best friend. All her ancestral luck as a leprechaun doesn't hurt either. When she takes a chance on an urgent client, the mysterious man at the heart of a scandal has her wondering how much longer she can keep herself a secret.

Leith Riordan just wants to drive boats by day and turn back into a merman at night—as simple as that. All his plans are destroyed, however, when a single lost temper lands him in a viral social media storm—and on Caiomhe Ryan's client roster. He knows his life can't go back to being simple. After all, it's not easy to tell a beautiful woman you're actually a merman.

Sparks fly and porridge burns when these two magical beings in the heart of Boston must decide if they can hide their real identity from the public while still being true to one another—and themselves.

Every Bite You Take

Bad Boy With a Heart of Gold, Woman In-Charge, Call Me a Good Girl, Caught in Public, Monster Romance, He Has How Many Eggplants?!, Whoops the Vampire is Hot, Woman Can't Choose So Tries Both, Fantasy Romance, Paranormal Romance

Evelyn Sharp thinks she's found her happy ending until a mysterious sea witch from Will's past appears and ruins everything.

Will Burleigh thought he'd found the key to breaking his curse—love and forgiveness from a human in the sexy and hilarious Evelyn. But his dark past quickly catches up to him when memories of his new life are erased, and he's returned to his dangerous, monstrous, former self.

Now, he must rely on his love to save him from future nightmares.

Dark truths are dragged into the light as two lovers learn to reconcile who they were with who they want to be. They say true love never runs smoothly, but is it supposed to be this bumpy?

Never Gonna Dig You Up

Coming home has never been so...dirty.

Billy Barlow lives a life his human self could've only dreamed of—luxury, women, wealth, ease. Vampirism has led to some major improvements. But when several local teens are injured on a real estate holding in the rural English village of Ashbourne, the town council demands he see to its repairs. What they don't know is that Billy is an Ashbourne local—from 200 years ago.

Leslee Hawthorne has all the talent and skill a hedge witch needs to land the honored title of Queen's Gardener. Too bad her ex-best friend has stolen credit and credence out from under her. When a slick, big-city guest arrives at the new hotel in town looking for someone to redo the Huxley Manor grounds on a minuscule timeline, Leslee thinks she's tripped into a major opportunity. If only she could focus on the task at hand and not on her new client's charming good looks.

All too soon, Leslee and Billy are forced together as they take on antiquated building laws, rogue teen vampires, and a mysterious creature terrorizing the village. But Billy's impulsive past actions catch up with him and Leslee will have to decide if she can cross the natural line she's sworn to uphold in the name of new love.

About the Author

Kel Bruem is a Bay Area-based indie monster romance author. Her Unusualities series include WHAT'S LUCK GOT TO DO WITH IT, EVERY BITE YOU TAKE, and NEVER GONNA DIG YOU UP. She is also an editor for the annual monster romance anthology TAILS, TRYSTS, & TENTACLES. When she's not writing, Kel trains her pit bull to be less stupid, explores new restaurants with her husband, and catches flights to her Sagittarian heart's content. You can find her online everywhere @kelbruem.

www.ingramcontent.com/pod-product-compliance
Lightning Source LLC
Chambersburg PA
CBHW060301310726

48976CB00007B/2162